Naomi Stewart

Destined To Dance

BY MARCY HEIDISH

A Woman Called Moses
a novel based on the life of Harriet Tubman

The Secret Annie Oakley
a novel based on the legendary sharpshooter

Witnesses
a novel based on the life of Anne Hutchinson

Miracles
a novel based on Mother Seton, first American Saint

Deadline
a novel of suspense

The Torching
a novel of supernatural suspense

A Dangerous Woman
Mother Jones, An Unsung American Heroine
a novel of a self-proclaimed Hell Raiser

ALSO BY MARCY HEIDISH

Who Cares? Simple Ways YOU Can Reach Out

A Candle At Midnight

Soul And The City

Defiant Daughters: Christian Women of Conscience

Destined To Dance

A Novel About Martha Graham

By Marcy Heidish

Dolan & Associates, Publisher

Destined To Dance

LIBRARY OF CONGRESS CATALOGING-IN-PUBLICATION DATA
Heidish, Marcy.

    p.cm.
    ISBN: 978-0-9831164-9-3
Library of Congress Control Number: 2011940376

Cover: Design and Original Art by Marcy Heidish

Dolan & Associates, Publisher

Printed in the United States of America

············

First edition

Dedicated To

All Who Seek A Life In The Arts

"When you do dance, I wish you
A wave o' th' sea, that you might ever do
Nothing but that."
  —Florizel, *The Winter's Tale (IV, iv, 159-161)*

PROLOGUE

Hades:

Sometime in the present.

My spirit is restless.

That's quite common here. Hades has never had a reputation as a spa. Not hell, not heaven, Hades is simply where the afterlife begins — for mortals with unfinished business. Once your earthly course is run, you bring that baggage here.

According to Greek myth, Hades is a neutral kind of place, known for its constant mists. I don't mind them. It's this endless beige decor that grows so tiresome. The ancient Greeks did not tell all.

This place has one requirement. It's the reason you're here. At some point, you must look back over your past. No exceptions. No cursory glances. The review is quite detailed. You may watch it in High Definition Color, if you want. No one does. The time of this event is left to you. Most of us put it off for centuries.

While you gather your nerve for this ordeal, your main activity is wandering. A stay in Hades is like extreme insomnia. In its advanced stages, you pace until dawn. Here the experience is much the same. Except, of course, there is no dawn. There are no exits, either. The beautiful Elysian Fields shimmer in the distance — out of bounds for now.

You can't reach them — or anywhere else — until you look back. You can't look back until you look within. You can't do that until you feel ready. At last I think I've reached that point. I've wandered enough since I arrived here in 1991. My time on earth lasted nearly ninety-seven years. I anticipate a lengthy viewing. I may as well get started now.

In life I was a pioneering dancer. I created a new "language" of movement, different from classical ballet. I left a school, a dance company, and 181 finished works. Some likened me to Picasso or Stravinsky — both here, of course, wandering together in the mists.Once we were hailed as geniuses. In this place we are no longer unique. Geniuses are plentiful in Hades.

Not so plentiful are brave souls, ready to look back. We sense what hindsight will entail. Graced moments will appear to us, of course. But we will see mistakes, missteps, missed chances, as well. Many viewers shriek, *What was I thinking*? We hear them as we wait our turn. I suspect I'll be one of those unquiet spirits.

Like everyone else here, I've left unfinished business behind. Not simply loose ends. My choices, I fear, have put my dance company in danger. Only after looking back can I intervene in some way — undisclosed, as yet. I hope my work outweighs my mistakes. It's hard to know what to expect. I'm traveling into uncharted territory. At least no wardrobe decisions are involved.

When I was fourteen, my family moved from east to west by rail. Thrilled, I ran through the entire train as it crossed the country. I ran through my life, at times, that way. Impulsive and intense, I welcomed new frontiers. Spirited and sensitive, I breathed in all I saw. That will serve me well, I hope, as I begin my review.

What comes back to me first? It is this singular image: A girl outside a cage. A girl with one black braid down her back. I remember when I wove my hair into that braid. I was eight years old that May.

Danger's beauty drew me then.

I was a girl who dared a god.

■

CHAPTER ONE

At eight, I locked eyes with a lion.

Fearless, entranced, I held his golden gaze. The great head leaned toward me and my small head leaned toward him. Did we stand there for an instant or infinity? I never was quite sure. It seemed to be the start of my life. It could have been the end of my life, too; I knew that.

This was not my first visit to the zoo or its wild beasts. Father had often brought me here with him.Only me; no one else. My father wanted to learn how animals spoke to one another through their movements. That would help him understand his patients who could not put their feelings into words. He was absorbed, lately, by tigers.

I slipped away. Always I returned to that one lion. As he paced, I watched the muscles rippling underneath his pelt. He was hot wax on glass; he was velvet over steel. His power coiled within him: a killer's power, perfectly controlled. God-like, he would never know fear; he would not allow his spirit to be caged.

The lion owned each step in his progression to the right and his progression to the left. And at each end, those wondrous turns, graceful, effortless. I longed to move like that, turn like that, walk like that.

Hypnotized, I drew closer to the cage.

That was when the lion turned to face me. He had always been aware of me, I knew. Now I felt his hot breath on my skin. He had tasted blood and honey; I smelled both. His topaz eyes looked at me and into me and through me with a timeless gaze. I drew closer still, aching to reach through the bars. For just a moment, I could put my hand out to the lion and —

I heard rapid footsteps coming toward me.

My father's steps. In haste, I drew back.

That was the last time I saw the lion. Life, then death, intervened. The next moment of equal intensity came to me in a frost-bitten field. There I went alone for absolution. That was not my only errand. I entered the field so I could send a message through the clouds.

~~~

Shouting to the midnight sky, I ran. The darkness opened out around me. Porous and protective, it absorbed my cries, *"Sorry sorry sorry."* At my mouth, white breath hovered like a bridal veil. My legs sliced air, my feet stamped earth, my hair streamed out behind me. I paused, listening, but heard no message of forgiveness. Head down, then, I plunged on ahead once more.

From the time I could remember, I had moved to the beat of my own pulse. Fast or slow, loud or soft, it prompted me, whatever my mood might be. Movement was my way of speaking when I lacked for words — and even when I didn't. I was grateful to this inner guide, this drumming self, for its steadfast loyalty. Now I listened for it once again to lead me through the dark.

No one was about, no one had spied my gown, an ivory blur against this balding field. A long expanse of naked earth, that space lay beyond the town and well beyond my father's sleeping house. It rested, all fires banked, all lamplight quenched, except within my father's study, where he nodded over his well-thumbed books of Greek mythology.

Unheard, unnoticed, I had slipped out the back door and darted away, leaving listeners behind. Now, at last, I was free to break into this run, this cry. I did not know where I was going; I did not need to know. Movement was my destination. Solitude, my sanctuary.

For me, there was always some relief from pain when I was in motion.

Damp air stroked my face and clasped my out-stretched hands, but the earth below me was not so forgiving. Autumn's first frost gripped this field tonight, stiffening small tufts of grass. They snatched at my hem and pricked my feet. I did not flinch, I did not cry out — this had to be the penitence I wanted. Through this green/gray field, I left a faint red trail like spilled wine. Blood was better than my mother's pointed sighs and ceaseless tears.

Now I hurtled forward, howling again, "*Sorry sorry sorry.*" Drawing air deep into my lungs I let loose another cry. Even if my throat turned raw, I must hurl my voice a mighty distance. I must get my words all the way to Heaven, where my younger brother had gone five days before; so the minister assured us at the funeral.

Gasping, bending over at the waist, I halted, wait-ing for some reply from above. "Won't you send a sign?" I called once more, then held myself so still I seemed to freeze in place. All I heard was my own harsh breathing and the wind rattling the bone-dry trees. "Forgive me," I whispered. "Forgive."

It seemed I crouched there a long time, alert to every sound or sign. Nothing. The wind dropped. The trees went still. The night was bigger than the ocean off the Jersey shore. There my family had one last holiday, two years earlier, before a new baby arrived —

the baby who was with us only eighteen months. The baby I now mourned out in the field.

~~~

I remember the day he was born. As soon as the midwife came to our house, my sisters and I were taken to a neighbor's home. We returned to joyous words: *A boy a boy a boy*! After three girls, here was the long awaited son at last, the only one who could place the Graham name beyond forgetting. From the bundle I once held in my arms, a tottering child had emerged, walking on his own, speaking new words every day. For eighteen months I had watched him grow — before the sickness came.

Why wouldn't he speak a word of comfort to his oldest sister now? *He died because of me*, that's why, I told myself. *It was all my fault.*

A month before the baby died, I had overheard my parents talking in the hall. I was sleepless, padding barefoot up the stairs. They were readying themselves for bed; the door to their room was ajar. I had heard them speak of my "strong will" before, but this time I caught the sounds of other words, as well. I could not have imagined them. Why would I ever want to hear them at all?

"The baby ..." Mother's voice. "My favorite."

"Oh, there's good in them all." Father's baritone.

"In Martha....?" A sigh. "Difficult from birth."

"Different...not 'difficult'....Sure to outgrow it."

"...even so. The boy's special to me...."

"Our son...." Father's voice. "What a kid."

"I shouldn't say...he makes up for *her*."

"Martha?" Father voice dropped.

They moved out of earshot then..

In the hall, I felt myself turn stiff and still. My forehead blazed, my hands felt hot against my face. Unbidden images rose within my brain. Forbidden images: My brother, in his crib, smothered with a giant feather pillow. Now *I* will be the favorite of all the Graham children.

How powerful were my thoughts? With my strong will, could I change events? Could my darkest will cause some calamity? Such an inner force frightened me. I must be wicked to harbor such evil ideas. In that fevered moment, I felt off-balance and unwell. The hall, oak floors, tea table, bunched roses, blue vase — everything blurred together. That night, I did not sleep.

The next day unfolded. Dawn. Cold sweat. Breakfast left untouched. Running from room to room, I tried to find my mother. The *Missus*, with the baby, had gone out, I was told. Calling on a neighbor, most likely, showing how her boy had grown. I waited at the window, listening for the horse's whinnies, the rattle of the returning carriage.

Questions. Swarming like gnats in July, so many questions. Had Mother hated me for ten whole years? To be exact, ever since May 11, 1894, when I was born?

Why? Had she taken an instant dislike to this baby with a head of ink black hair? A colicky baby, always screaming, always crying, shattering the household's peace. I knew the story, told and retold, until it was imprinted on my brain:

Mother could not manage me as an infant, longer than two weeks. That was when Elizabeth Prendergast appeared at the front door, summoned by my father. Well-known to him, ginger-haired, large and capable, "Lizzie" was quick to announce her name and her mission: "The doctor sent me to help." My young mother thrust her baby into Lizzie's arms. "Just *take* her," Jenny Graham had blurted out. Lizzie did. And stayed to raise us all.

~~~

I had my father's love, I knew, but my sisters seemed closer to mother. How pretty they were, Mother told "her girls." And so they were, with curling auburn hair, hazel eyes and creamy skin with cheeks the color of ripe apricots. Perhaps they favored our father's Irish ancestors. Then again, they might favor Mother's stock, proud descendants of the Mayflower Puritans. This question could be relied upon to set off heated debates.

Like our father, my sister Mary was tall, with long legs. Geordie, the youngest, was already a beauty. I sometimes longed to muss their hair. Their clothes were never soiled. They were so well-behaved, they made me want to scream. Plain, dark, and short, I seemed to spring from some other family. My intensity and restlessness set me apart from my sedate sisters. But I found compensations.

Plain or not, I was the eldest and the strongest of the threesome. This entitled me, I felt, to devise games for the younger girls. After Lizzie told us about Dublin's Abbey Theatre, I was too excited for sleep. I planned my own amateur "theatricals" and meted out my sisters' roles. Lizzie's stories, Father's myths, and Mother's Shakespeare sparked my imagination. I made costumes and wrote scripts, enacted by the three of us, always under my direction. I was the boss there, if no where else. We were strictly forbidden to wear our costumes downstairs.

Like our mother, my younger sisters always wore their cotton gloves and veils outside. This was customary attire for well-bred females in the Allegheny Valley, where coal dust always permeated the air. Proper ladies must take proper measures, we Graham girls were told. As usual, I took such proper measures, but handled them a bit differently.

I was always losing my gloves or kicking them under my bed. The veil was different. Draped over the head, it carried an aura of mystery, drawn from Dickens and Sir Walter Scott. When I wore my veil indoors and wafted about the house, I could be a noblewoman in disguise or an emissary on a secret errand....

But not for long.

"No veils indoors," Mother snapped. "Off!"

"Everything looks different through the mesh—"

"What's wrong with you?" My mother sighed.

"I was just—" I did not know the answer.

"Why can't you be more like your sisters?"

"I'm...myself." I was tired of this question.

"Indeed. You resemble no one in *this* family."

"Mother, may I start ballet lessons with Mary?"

"Not you. *Your* legs are too short for dancing."

I ran outside to the ancient oak tree; I had often sought refuge there. Some of the broad branches were in easy reach. A reader from an early age, I liked to climb a low bough with a book. The Bronte sisters' novels were the ones I favored at the time. Just now, though, I needed to move.

From my pocket, I drew out a long coiled rope. A few minutes later, I heard my mother scream my name. I glanced down from the tree's lowest bough. Below me, Mother stood frozen, it seemed, hands on hips, horror on her face. To be polite, I stopped what I was doing and let the rope dangle from my fingers.

"It's fine, Mother. I always stay balanced."

"Skipping rope? In a tree? Is fine? *Get down.*"

"Yes, Ma'am." I leapt to the ground. "I—"

"No excuses. Is it sense you lack — or is it fear?"

My eyes blazed. "Probably it's...both."

"I said, 'Don't be fresh?' What gets into you?"

"Nothing." I waited for the inevitable question.

"Why on earth can't you be like your sisters?"

That question had become more frequent after a certain incident in church. Strict Presbyterians, we Grahams always sat in the same pew and one Sunday, I had disgraced my family. Seven years old, in white organdy with matching hair ribbons, I burst from our pew and danced up the empty center aisle to a favorite hymn. My mother had blanched. Presbyterians did not dance, let alone in church. Proper ladies did not dance at all, anywhere — nor did their daughters.

~~~

Now, three years later, I felt a strong need to talk with my mother. I had to know if she really loved me, after all. I had to know if she'd really meant what she'd said to my father that night.

As I came upstairs, I heard a woman's laughter floating from the bathroom down the hall. There was a splash of water. More laughter. A small voice like a penny whistle. A swish, a whoop, my mother's voice, clearer now.

"Ooop-la, up we go, my darling boy."

Snapping cloth: A towel?

"Ma...ma, ma...ma—."

"Let's not get chilled."

Unnoticed, I had shifted my position to the open bathroom door. Within, the walls were painted the fragile blue of the sky at dawn. The claw-foot tub, scrubbed to a shine, resembled a ballet slipper. Ivory curtains stirred above the tub — careless as usual, I had forgotten to close that window when I'd washed my hands before noon dinner.

Never mind, I told myself. On their rack, the plush towels looked bosomy and comforting. One already wrapped the baby, enthroned on Mother's lap. Beneath them, a low rocking chair creaked in a steady rhythm. *One...and two...and one...and....* Wriggling, the baby laughed louder, the reedy notes rising to a joyous shriek.

Mother was kissing him, starting upward from the belly, moving to the chest and face, and each kiss made a funny smacking sound. He seemed to dance with laughter until, suddenly, in rapid succession, three sneezes burst from him.

Mother frowned. "God bless, God bless...."

"God...dess," the baby repeated every sound.

"All dry now. Yes? Time for your sweet lotion?"

"Yes, yes, yes" the baby crowed.

"Love you, love you best, don't tell, our secret..."

The baby sneezed again and stopped his chatter.

"Oh no." Mother paused. "Window's open."

"I'll close it for you." From the doorway I spoke.

Mother's eyes were gray, metallic, cold.

"Martha, y*ou* left that window open?"

Saying nothing, I moved to lower the sash.

"You should answer your elders."

My throat had closed. "I do," I choked out.

"Now he's shivering...If he gets sick..."

With one stricken look, I fled the room.

Twenty-four hours later, the baby's skin had passed from warm to hot to flushed; his labored breathing could no longer be dismissed. Several times Father listened to his son's small chest with a gleaming stethoscope, with his stethoscope. Mother hovered near the crib and wound folds of her silken skirts around her hands.

Watching Father's face, I knew before he told her. A psychiatrist, he was called an "Alienist" — his era's term for members of his chosen profession. For more than two decades, he had only treated patients with mental disorders; too many years had passed since he had dealt with physical ailments. He could do nothing for his own child now.

It was time to call a specialist, he said.

Just to be on the safe side; he repeated that.

It was clear to me: my father had detected some disturbance in the baby's chest.

I wanted to hide, I wanted to scream, I wanted to run. Most of all, I wanted to pour my strong clean breath into the baby's bud-like mouth. My younger sisters looked pale and paralyzed. I took a step toward the crib. My mother stopped me with a look.

The specialist arrived. Looking down the stairwell, I could see his black bowler hat and furled umbrella. With chilling calm, he moved up the steps. His left shoe squeaked as he ascended; I always remembered that. He seemed to linger in the baby's room for hours, but I watched the hall clock. He had only stayed for nine minutes. Father paced as the two men conferred downstairs; I heard familiar steps. After the doctor left with his ominous bag and his opaque smile, our house fell under a spell of solemn silence.

Voices were lowered. Steps were muted. Doors stayed shut. In the kitchen, pans did not clank at stove or sink. No one spoke at meals; the only sounds were the chink of knives and forks. Lizzie went about her baking, but her green eyes glimmered with tears.

It was she who usually bathed the baby and she always checked the window first. Last Thursday, on her day off, she was trying on a hat while the baby splashed in the huge tub, pristine as a pearl — positioned in a draft. Now I watched Lizzie take her baked bread from the oven. I ran upstairs to be sick in the sink.

Finally, the baby's diagnosis was announced. I felt the terror on the air inside our house. My brother had contracted...a terrible pause...rheumatic fever: two words feared by every parent. No one said those five syllables out loud; they were always whispered.

At that time, rheumatic fever was incurable. There were no medicines to fight it. Herbal brews never worked. Death was the usual outcome. Some children were strong enough to fight the fever, but their hearts were often damaged and, in most cases, they did not have long lives. Nothing could be done. Nothing except hope and prayer, Lizzie murmured.

"Sometimes it's mild." Father spoke in the large voice he only used out of doors. "Everything will be just fine." Now he was indoors, closing up his offices downstairs. All consultations had been canceled for a week. The house had to be quiet now.

~~~

Twelve years earlier, Father had gone into private practice, using wasted space in his own home. He rarely talked about his years as a physician at a mental hospital: a place filled with noise, he once said — and stopped. Even here, downstairs, some patients raised their voices. This fascinated me, but frightened my sisters. When a shriek rose from the rooms below, Geordie would run into the broom closet.

Now, I thought, this heavy silence was far worse than noises below. Upstairs the air felt heavier than before a thunder storm. "Count your blessings — or else," Grandmother had often warned us with an eerie sense of cheer. Her voice always brightened when she spoke of Divine retribution and eternal damnation. I ran to Lizzie in the kitchen.

Her face, usually ruddy, had lost its color, but her strong frame did not bend or tremble. Big, freckled, and sensible, she was a hill of a woman, earthy and eternal, outlasting any weather. Lizzie had lived through hard times in Ireland but seldom spoke of them. Instead, she wove tales of a green land, home to a race of magical people. Some of these were mischievous; others changed their shape at will. There was a saint named Brigid who turned water into beer; and a daring pirate woman called Grainne. And there were more....

I was easily entranced and quieted by stories. Lizzie never reprimanded me for misbehavior; instead, the wise woman simply engaged my imagination. Now Lizzie moved two kitchen chairs into a spill of buttery light, sat me down, and began another tale.

Listening to Lizzie, I felt myself grow calmer. For an hour, I forgot about my brother's fever. When the story ended, Lizzie held me, and together we swayed back and forth together in a rocking chair. I went over every word of these folk tales. I carried them away from the kitchen, held them in my mind, and stored them in my memory for comfort.

I would need it.

~~~

The next day the air seemed to darken our house. There was a change in my brother's breathing, though it didn't take a specialist to hear it. There was an increasingly erratic pulse in my brother's chest — I overheard the doctor's latest report. My parents and my grandmother stationed themselves at the baby's crib and, as if on cue, Lizzie herded us girls into the nursery.

From our window we could see the minister arrive: black suit, steel-rimmed spectacles, prayer book in hand. The hall clock chimed the quarter hour. And then a wail — *"NoNoNoNoNo"* — from my brother's room. "Put him down, Jenny," Father's voice was firm. Lizzie crossed herself and stopped the pendulum in the great hall clock.

Suddenly, the expansive house seemed unfamiliar. Weeping filled the air like falling snow. Two men arrived, one with the small coffin in his arms; the other, in a black suit, with a satchel. He did his work and, on his way out, he laid his card on the silver tray on the hall table. For the first time, I saw tears in my father's eyes.

Doors opened and shut. Large as trays, pies began to load the kitchen table. In the silent upstairs hall, footsteps clicked. There were murmurs outside my mother's room. She had closed the door and taken to her bed when the mortician left. Friends left notes and flowers at the bedroom's threshold, but the door remained unopened.

In the nursery, my sisters and I clung to Lizzie. She smoothed our hair and rubbed our cold hands. Finally, she took us with her to "that place." It was a secret, cherished and well-kept. The light, the scent, the serenity of Lizzie's Catholic church always calmed and thrilled us. Today, we would do something new. Each of us would go to the bank of votive candles and light one for our brother.

"After you leave here," Lizzie said, "your prayer will go on dancing in that tiny flame."

My love of ritual started in that little Catholic church, scented with incense, flowers, floor polish, and tallow. I always remembered High Mass in this sanctuary. Red/blue/golden light spilling through the windows; richly colored vestments spread like wings as the priest raised his arms. *Oremus....* A visit to Lizzie's church always seemed to push back the darkness, within and without, and so it did that day.

~~~

But what day was it? Time began to blur. Was it Thursday now, or Friday? *Wednesday's child was full of woe, Thursday's child had a long way to go....* The death was Wednesday, then. Lizzie served sliced ham, "funeral ham," she called it as they did in Ireland. She baked large batches of small cookies: "Wake cakes," she said they were. Grandmother would have had a stroke if she'd known Irish Catholic customs had penetrated this Protestant home. I had to smile at that thought — my only smile for many days. The funeral would be tomorrow.

I remembered little of the burial. Only the small coffin and the preacher's frequent references to hell. Be thankful, he exhorted us. This baby would escape

much of hell's pains by dying before he could err —
though he still must pay for Original Sin.

Watching my grandmother's nod at each pro-
nouncement, I made a silent decision: I would never be
like her. I would not become that woman with the grim
eyes and the granite heart. *So help me, God*, I sealed
my vow. The preacher went on but I did not listen
anymore. Rage got me through the service, the burial,
and the "reception" afterwards.

Then, even worse, there was the silent aftermath:
A glimpse of the empty crib. A rocking chair. A blue
blanket; a tin soldier on its side. Lizzie's broad hands
led me away. The next day, another glimpse: the
baby's room, now stripped and bare. Smells of lye soap
and acrid smoke.

A small mattress burning outside, well behind the
house; Father looking on, a rake in one hand. Upstairs Mother wept and kept to her room. Every day,
when Lizzie led us girls in to say, "Good Morning,"
there was no answer, only fresh tears. I touched my
mother's hand. She jerked her hand away.

~~~

And so, I slipped out at night into the field.

The darkness remained permeable as water, giving
me the space to run and run and run, shouting out my
"*Sorries*." My limbs flexed and bent and moved,
bearing me across the frost-struck field. But at its far

end, I stopped short. An image of my brother in his coffin rose into my mind.

I felt a sob deep within my gut. It wrenched me; it seemed about to break me in two. For a moment, I was unable to breathe ... and then I released a stream of air. I felt the sobbing ease. Exhausted, I squatted on the ground, letting the tears come. How had I held all of them inside so long?

Retracing my steps, I was wary as I neared our house. In this safest suburb, a fair distance from Pittsburgh, people often left their homes unlocked. If no one awakened, I could easily slip through the back door — but now, I paused.

Through the kitchen window, I saw someone moving about. I knew this tall, rangy silhouette as well as I knew my own reflection. I had not antici-pated father's penchant for late-night sweets. The back door opened onto a small mud-room leading to the spacious kitchen. This entry was off-limits to me now.

I hesitated, nervous, bouncing on the balls of my feet. In a moment, my decision made, I moved around the property to the north side of the house. Here, on the lowest floor, I saw the dark windows of my father's consultation rooms. This section of the house had a separate entrance, only used by patients, never bolted. I approached the door. Silently, its knob rotated in my hand. The door swung open into a dark passageway. I stepped inside and listened.

Abruptly, then, I heard footsteps coming down the back stairs. Those were my father's brisk steps.

Without time to think, I darted into an empty consultation room. Scarcely breathing, I flattened myself against its wall. The footsteps hesitated, then moved down the hall toward my father's lamplit study.

My knees went watery and I sat hard, too hard, in the nearest chair. The frost-bound field seemed dreamlike now; its wind, too, seemed imaginary. *This* was real. This was the house where my brother's heart had fluttered to a stop. This was the house where the doctor and the mortician had arrived in black bowler hats. This was the house where I had once twirled with my brother in my arms.

Guilt spiraled through me once again. Finally defeated, head bent, knees to chest, I rocked back and forth. Something sour rose in my throat. I choked it down and closed my eyes. My only refuge was this rhythmic movement.

Now, in the empty consultation room, I jumped. An oil lamp swung into sight, hanging in the doorway like a misplaced moon. Trembling, I saw my father's hand and face illuminated by the lamp he held. Saying nothing, he scanned my torn night shift, my soiled and bloody feet, my tangled hair.

I wondered if I looked worse than any patient ever had, sitting in this room, this wicker chair. That question was too terrible to ask. I feared its answer. Father set the lamp on a low table and pulled up another chair so he could face me. With his large warm hands he covered my cold fingers. When he spoke he did not scold; his voice was mild.

"Where did you go, dear Martha?"

"The garden. Walking. I got dirty."

"Somehow I don't think so," he smiled.

"Maybe you just couldn't see me."

"Maybe you were somewhere else."

Tears came then. "How did you know?"

"You make fists when you tell...fibs."

"Yes." I noticed my clenched hands.

"You look down. Can't meet my eyes."

"You always said, 'The body never lies.' "

I unclenched my fists. And abruptly, hard words tumbled out of me at last. The field. The run. The shouts of regret, the pleas for forgiveness.

"No answer." I went slack. "I called and called."

"Were you expecting words?" My father asked.

"Well, I mean, I hoped for them. I listened."

"Did you tell that lion how you felt about him?"

"No." My head lifted. "I didn't say a thing."

"Then why expect an answer in words now?"

I looked into my father's face. "I guess...I can't."

"Next time you go out at night, tell me first."

"Yes." The air between us warmed. "I'm sorry."

"I am. You were afraid of me, my beautiful girl."

"Not me." I burst out. "I'm no one's beautiful girl."

Father looked at me. "Why do you say that?"

"I'm bad." I buried my head in my knees again. "I left the window open in the bathroom."

"You think you caused your brother's death? Drafts don't bring on rheumatic fever, Martha."

"You don't know what I wished." I looked down.

Slowly, Father drew out the whole story.

"Martha. Listen. *You can't will someone to die.*"

"Even though I'm always called 'strong-willed'?"

"*Even so. You did not kill your brother.* Hear me?"

I nodded. Some inner vise let go, releasing me. I breathed in air I never tasted before. There were no words now, only breath. Through the open window came the sound of crickets. Night birds called. The world started to turn again — then halted in its new rotation. How could I stay here if my mother hated me, Grandmother, too?

Struggling, I told my father what I'd overheard that evening in the hall outside my parents' room — the words prompting my death-wish.

The expression on my father's face startled me. Always calm and peaceable, my father suddenly appeared enraged, ashamed, agonized.

I looked away from him; such clashing emotions seem to warrant privacy. I glanced around this room where my father worked with children. My own rag dolls look down from its shelves. There was a plush lamb, an Easter gift, and wooden blocks, and my father's old tin soldiers. A sudden terror struck me then; I broke into my father's private thoughts.

"Am I crazy, like the children who come here?"

"They're not crazy. *Neither are you.* Hear me?"

I let out my breath. "What am I, then?"

"Right now? Troubled. Grieving. Misunderstood." He sighed. "That was wrong of us to speak that way, your mother and I. I'm sorry, Martha. I knew better. Mother's still so very young. I've got fifteen years on her, you know." He winked, then, his face relaxing. "And remember, I said nothing about *my* favorite child."

I flew to him then, leaning into his smell of pipe-smoke, shaving soap and mentholated cough drops. Even so, I knew the moment I left his arms, I would backslide into disbelief again. I'd heard too much over the years about my strong-willed ways. I'd seen a darkness in myself these last few days, a darkness never quite revealed to me before.

"You're still not sure," my father said.

"I *want* to believe you," I punched each word out.

My father sighed. "One day, I hope you will."

"Sometimes I'm afraid of this power inside me."

"Use it, then, for the good. Build. Love. Bless."

"I wish ... I could tell the baby how I feel."

"Show him." My father nodded. "Can you do that?"

I looked around the room once more. Finally I took a rag doll off the shelf. I knew this doll; I'd slept with its soft bulk for years. Soft bulk like a baby's. Closing my eyes, I began to sway with the small bundle in my arms.

Step and step and lean and turn... One movement flowed into another, forming a slow dance, improvised as I went along.

I spun a sacred circle on the air. No misery could touch me here. No human could bestow this magic.

Where could I find it once again?

■

CHAPTER TWO

My father introduced me to the goddess.

First, came the violets — still moist as he pinned them to my plain gray dress. Next, he presented me with a round box, lifted out a new hat, and set it at a rakish angle on my head. I could only gasp my thanks.How could I deserve this? My birthday was coming, my father said. He might be away; we would celebrate today.

And then he led me toward the moment that divided and defined my life. It was seventeen days before my seventeenth birthday: I have always remembered the exact date: the Twenty-Fourth of April, 1911.I also remembered the setting for this introduction: The Mason Opera House in downtown Los Angeles, California.

Looking back, it seems inevitable that I would reach that magical oasis. I willed myself to penetrate a dream. At the time, the pattern may have seemed coincidental, but in fact, I was closing in on this destination as if it had been waiting all along for my arrival.

I can calculate my journey's starting point with the sort of clarity you rarely find in life. My first step came in 1908, when Father moved our family to Santa Barbara, California. Its climate would be healthier for everyone, especially Mary, my middle sister, who was prone to asthma. No one was sorry to leave the Allegheny Valley. No one regretted those veils, thrown into the dustbin, or the thick dim air, forgotten.

In Santa Barbara, I had far more space to move about outside — without gloves or veils. I remember running with my sisters, screaming with laughter: falling, scrambling, running on again. Flowers were lush, reds were redder, the air was warm. The sun seemed closer in California.

With my father, I watched families of dolphins dive and dart through the blue/green waters near the our new home. And just three hours south was the great city of Los Angeles with its palm trees, broad avenues, theatres, shops and music halls.

Father asked me to describe the City of the Angels in one word. No single word seemed big enough to me. *"Swell,"* I said at last, giving out the highest term of praise existing in America that year. And, I knew, something extraordinary was going to happen to me there. My intuitions tended to be right. I only had to force myself to wait for whatever might be coming.

It was in Los Angeles that the goddess first appeared to me. Walking with my parents through the city, I saw a poster in a shop's front window. I came to an abrupt stop. From the poster a woman's face gazed out at me and into me and through me, with a smile. The face was lovely and exotic, framed by streams of golden gauze, blending with long skirts. Was this Madonna or Minerva? I could not look away.

The renowned dancer, Ruth St. Denis, was posed and dressed as Radhu, a Hindu deity, sparkling in silks and jewels. Soon she would give a performance in Los Angeles. I asked my father if he would take me to the show. Did I catch a frown from my mother? It didn't matter. What counted was my father's ready "Yes." He went up to the city often and looked forward to catching a show there with his favorite daughter.

Just the way a gentleman would escort a lady, he took my arm as we entered the opera house. I caught a whiff of violets from my corsage as we progressed down the red-carpeted aisle. We found our seats, front and center. The place itself looked magical, decorated like an ornate Indian temple — or how I imagined such a temple would look. Above my head, chandeliers sparkled and swayed. I was awestruck well before the performance could begin.

Slowly, then, the house lights went down. A hush fell over the hall. I remember the skin prickling at the nape of my neck; I scarcely breathed. The crimson curtains parted in a majestic folds as it drew back. And center stage, bathed in light and seated on a golden box, there she was: The goddess.

Layers of tangerine gauze draped her graceful figure. Dozens of rings glittered on her spread fingers. Surrounded by waves of incense, she uncoiled her long legs and rose, and rose, and rose, until the goddess seemed about to levitate. Instead, she began to sway, her arms outstretched like wings. A layer of lime gauze appeared, swaying with her as if she could generate her own breeze.

Now she did a series of stunning turns, sending her long skirts outward in widening circles. Ruth St. Denis was gone. In her place was Radhu, the gracious Hindu deity, blessing earth and sky. Each step was graceful, each gesture was smooth. Flutes and chimes blended together in some kind of celestial music. The woman's dance unfurled like silk.

Another number followed, then another, each separated from the other by repeated curtain calls. When it was all over, I could not move. I remained in my seat until my father laid a gentle hand on me. Still tranced, I rose but paused again, staring at the crack where the curtains met. I had found the image I'd hoped to find. Here it was.

And at that moment, I *knew*. Just *knew*.

My life, I felt, was sealed. I was destined to dance. I had been summoned by the goddess. Of course, this secret had to be well kept for now. I would know when it was time to reveal my calling. Until then, I would prepare for my vocation. To start with, I quit the high school basketball team and all other sports that posed a threat to my legs.

~~~

Meanwhile, my family was planning my higher education. A fine selection of women's colleges were proposed. Instead of Vassar or Wellesley, my parents' preferences, I chose The Cumnock School of Expression, also in Los Angeles. This junior college had a liberal arts curriculum which pleased my father. Perhaps my parents did not hear about the school's emphasis on the performing arts. One of its featured courses was "Interpretive Dance" — three times a week.

When I made my choice, I did not know another institution was soon to open. It would be the first professional school of dance in America. Based in Los Angeles, the school was planned as a residential facility for those gifted enough to be admitted. The setting would be conducive to artistic spirits: A grove of fragrant eucalyptus trees surrounding a rambling Spanish mansion, ancient but refurbished, with an air of grandeur, character, and history.

Inside there would be ample studio space, as well as rooms for students. The school would attract the most talented dancers with its faculty and its renowned musical director. Outside there would be a vast lawn, fragrant with flowers, where tame peacocks could open their iridescent tails. This was the vision of a well-known dancer, Ted Shawn, and his wife, Ruth St. Denis herself. This oasis would be known as Denishawn.

Even if I had known about this haven, Cumnock must come first, I knew. My father felt strongly about its careful supervision of young ladies in their dorms. The curriculum pleased him: classes in poetry, mythology, and playwriting. He wanted me to be grounded in the classics before I moved forward into my life. This, he knew, would differ from the expected patterns suited to his other girls.

"I only want the best for you," my father told me, echoing the words of every parent to a growing daughter. "Only the best, Martha, you know that."

On a weekend visit home, toward the end of my first year at college, I sat up late with Father. He hoped I would go on to get my degree from Cumnock. And then? I did not see myself as wife or mother — at least, not yet. I had no romantic interests at the moment anyway. Father seemed to understand and did not press me about subjects so sensitive and personal as romance.

"But you're holding back," he told me.

"You always know." My clenched hands had given me away.

The house was quiet. We were sitting in the family's wood-paneled kitchen: a comfortable room with ladder-back chairs, a broad table, a copper bowl of oranges set on a blue cloth. I peeled an orange, letting its fragrance fill the air as I spoke of Denishawn, open to new students. My words fluttered with excitement. This place was now my obsession — and my goal.

"Denishawn....?" Father repeated. "Odd name."

"Remember Ruth St. Denis? The opera house?"

"Of course. I've wondered what you took from it."

"I knew then." I sighed. "I had to dance. I feel...."

"...that power we talked about? I remember."

"Like a lion's power, caged. But bigger, infinite."

"Denishawn channels this through dance?"

I nodded. "If they take me. If you'd let me try...?"

Thinking, my father paused, a bit short of breath.

"Try," he said then. "After Cumnock. Is that fair?"

"Oh God, thank you — Father — Father?"

He rose, gripping his left arm; his face was ashen. "*Damn,*" he muttered. Trying to steady himself, he over-turned one of the chairs. "*Not now,*" he said through clenched teeth. "*Not yet.*" He doubled over, grabbing the edge of the kitchen table.

"Tell me what to do," I reached for him. "*Tell me.*"

His hand moved to his chest; he stared at me.

"*Not* your fault. Remember," he grimaced.

"Don't go." I felt the room begin to spin. "Hold on."

"Listen. Do what we said. Promise."

"Promise. But please, let me get help—"

"Must be... strong. Manage. Your mother can't —"

He reached upwards, grabbed a handful of air, and crumpled to his knees. *"Stay,"* I begged, cradling his head in my lap. His eyelids flickered as his breathing rattled. A moment later, he was gone.

During the next week I silently repeated his words to myself like a chant, a prayer, an invocation. *Not your fault, remember.* These words rolled through my mind like beads as I went about my tasks. *Manage.... Must be strong...must must must....*

And I did manage, leaning on that sturdy hill of a woman, Lizzie Prendergast. Staunch, postponing tears, she baked rolls, made beds, brewed tea, said her Rosary and, with me, lit a dozen votive candles. Arrangements were made. Relatives were assembled. And at last, the ordeal was over. The funeral ended with the hymn, *Blest Be The Tie That Binds.*

The prayer of committal had been offered. The minister had raised his hand over the mourners. *May the Lord bless you and keep you.* My mother, supported by her younger daughters, wavered on her feet. *May the Lord lift up his countenance upon you....* The hearse was gone; black cars idled just outside the cemetery's gates.... *And grant you peace.*

After everyone had left the grave, I darted back for one private moment. I still could not believe I'd never hear my father's voice again. How could he be lying in the earth beneath my feet? Would his spirit stay with me somehow? No message came to me, no matter how I prayed for one. *Did you expect an answer in words?*

It seems a long time since my father had asked me that. But now I felt his presence; now I heard his voice in my head and in my spirit. There were no words big enough to express the way I felt. Before I went back to the house, I left a bowl of oranges on the mound of freshly spaded earth.

At home, I opened my father's closet. His suits and shirts hung, ready to be worn. Abruptly, I felt a chill sweep over my skin; a sign of shock, I knew. Wasn't that to be expected now? I'd not stopped moving for five days. Now was not the time to sort out clothes and shoes and cuff links. I grabbed my father's dressing gown and went down to his office. There, I nestled into the settee where Father used to sit and read, often in this dressing gown. The scent of his shaving soap, pipe smoke and cough drops still clung to it.

My father had been a tall man; this garment was far too big for the small girl I was. Like a blanket, though, it could enfold me. I wrapped myself in the dressing gown until I was almost covered. Still I shivered; the anguish, held off for so long, had taken over. I thrashed there, wrestling with the pain before it paralyzed me. I must "manage;" I must return to school.

Grief is so useless, I thought. *But if it's so useless, why is it so strong?* I would have liked to ask my father that. He alone would know the answer. I could not guess the answer's seed already lay within me.

~~~

Nearly ten years later, my mentor Louis Horst was standing in the first wing of a Manhattan theatre, watching the answer unfold. It was a chilly night in January but the house was filling for a premiere: Martha Graham's latest dance solo, simply titled, *Lamentation.*

Louis wondered if I shouldn't call it *Immolation.* That's what I was risking with this new creation. Of course, I would not listen to anyone, let alone to reason. I insisted on trying the unthinkable in public, gambling with my reputation. I wanted to dance this solo — *seated.*

Who the hell could dance while sitting down? Louis muttered in the wings. Would this notion break my winning streak with the critics? Or perhaps, we'd write it off as an experiment or headline their review with some cute phrase like *Consternation.* What if I got boos or jeers or, far worse, laughter? Could such a sensitive soul bear public rejection?

Often anguished about my own creations, I had an eerie confidence about this one. The stage was bare. The music, by the great Hungarian composer Zoltán Kodály, was somber yet sublime. The costume was my own design. *"Saints preserve us,"* Lizzie said before she joined the audience. She saw what "her girl" had come up with now. In my favorite shop on the lower East Side, I had selected yards of cotton tricot, a new material at that time.

Then I had the tricot shaped into a tube-like wrap enclosing my body from head to ankles, with openings for face and hands and feet. Depending on the way I moved under the lights, the fabric appeared to be lavender, violet, and plum. Just before the curtain rose, I arranged myself inside this material and sat center stage on a low bench. No one else could have carried it off, Louis said later: No one else could have made tricot tubing move with eloquence. The design was elegant as well and soon inspired copies.

The material behaved exactly as I knew it would. It conformed to my torso and my limbs, yet the tube was large enough to let me move within it. The curtain, going up, revealed a classic figure of sorrow, and the costume was my dance partner: The audience gave a collective gasp.

Now, inside this purple cocoon, I began to move, rotating and bending in grief. My face was anguished but I let my body speak. It expressed the pain of loss and the human need to strain against it. Writhing, turning, I was enveloped in my shroud of sorrow, aching to escape.

I thrust one hand outward. Then one bare foot, stretching in another direction. This was Jacob wrestling with the angel; this was Rachel agonizing over her lost children. This was Mary at the foot of the Cross. The critics said the movements were excruciating and exquisite; there was a strange beauty in this picture of grief. The stricken figure, I was told, looked like a Rodin sculpture in motion. With each rotation, each bent knee or elbow, the fabric changed shape. The silent mourner could find no relief — only emotional release.

There was a hush before the applause began and crested, coming at me in waves, and then there was the cry for curtain calls. Louis mopped his forehead and lit a fresh cigar. Everyone backstage was lightened, giddy, laughing with relief — toasting that unknown genius, the inventor of cotton tricot. Finally I made my way back to my dressing room. At its door, a weeping woman awaited "Madame Dancer."

The house manager had told the visitor to wait outside, but I drew her into that *sanctum sanctorum* and held her as she sobbed out her story: Months earlier her young son had been hit by a car and killed. Even after weeks of shock, the stricken woman had been unable to grieve, to sleep, to accept her loss — until this evening's performance. "You have no idea what you've done for me," she told me. "And I thank you."

I've never said anything about my own experience with grief. I've never spoken of my father's death. It took years, but at last I did speak of loss to everyone who witnessed *Lamentation.* Wherever I danced it, the ballet called forth strong emotional responses. This piece was germinating in me when I finally arrived at Denishawn — that place of destiny.

■

CHAPTER THREE

Everything looks different from Hades.

You see the bones within the body. You see events stripped of illusions. Not at all the way life appears as you live it. In 1916, the time I'm viewing now, I thought Denishawn would be my home forever. I could not know it was a stop along the way. Nor could I know it would end in flames, torched by its founders when they parted.

To me, at first, Denishawn was an eternal Eden — and so it was for other young dancers. It was *the* place to be, to learn, to launch a career. I was young when I first arrived there, younger than I realized, and I gazed around like Dorothy in Oz.

~~~

Denishawn.

Eucalyptus trees and peacocks.

Piano music floating out the windows.

Inside: Smell of roses, incense, sweat.

At last I was there. I couldn't quite believe it. Every morning as I woke, I feared I'd find myself back in Santa Barbara or worse, Pittsburgh. I had waited a year for this chance. Even six months earlier my solo debut would have been unthinkable.

Denishawn had all the marks of a winner: success, ecstatic press, and a growing reputation. It outshown Isadora Duncan's ground-breaking work in modern dance, which was, in any case, restricted to Europe. Denishawn, not Duncan, attracted hundreds of American students who vied for its limited placements. Interviews alone were hard to get; it was harder still to win acceptance from Miss Ruth and her husband, dancer/choreographer Ted Shawn. Few applicants lived up to their standards and entered this elite new school.

I nearly didn't make the cut myself. When I appeared for my final audition, the place was overbooked and understaffed. The audition schedule was backed up. Everyone was tired and out of sorts. The last applicant that day, I was in a state of high anxiety after my long wait. My future mentor and musical guru, Louis Horst, happened to be there. He confirmed my frank assessment of my Denishawn audition. I summed it up in one word, easy to say, but difficult to swallow: *DISASTER.*

I was in awe of "Miss Ruth:" the goddess herself, even more enchanting in person. The famous dancer's fine-boned face was set off by a crown of premature white hair. It seemed to smoke from her head like incense, and the scent of sandalwood hung heavy in the air. St. Denis wore a loose-fitting silvery blouse, exposing her midriff, heavy silver bracelets on her languid arms, and a long skirt, also silvery, which swept the floor as she moved. To me, she was a celestial vision.

Ted Shawn, rehearsing their touring company, was not present till the end of my audition. I was alone with the pianist — and the goddess. Around me, the studio seemed to open out like a wheat field. A wall of mirrors made the room seem even larger: Two wheat-fields. There was a cluster of Ficus trees, a ballet barre, and in one corner, a baby grand piano.

The man behind it seemed absorbed in a paperback thriller. Portly, broad-shouldered, fortish, he had a cigar clamped in his teeth. His world-weary air was customary. Sighing, he marked his place, set aside his novel and glanced over at me. He did not glance away. How small I must have appeared, adrift in that big room. As Louis noted, I looked like a child lost in a big city department store.

I had prepared — and practiced — a sequence from Cumnock's classes in "Interpretive Dance." Before I could offer the pianist the music, he began to play a Viennese waltz. "Why did you do that to me, Louis?" I asked him later. "I thought you would know all about the waltz," he said. "I wanted to make things easier on you. After all, you looked so stricken."

A strict Presbyterian upbringing ruled out ball-room dancing. Even so, that waltz went on while I flailed about, struggling with its rhythm and its tempo. Miss Ruth cut off the audition. She had seen more than enough. This girl, she must have thought, was wasting everybody's time. I sensed my idol's scorn and felt my stomach turn over. The pianist sent me a sympathetic glance drew on his cigar.

"Our musical director," Miss Ruth nodded at him. "Louis Horst."

"Delighted." He bowed. "And you are....?"

Finished, I thought. *Done.* "Miss Graham. Again?"

"No." The goddess yawned. "Let me look at you."

"Should I stand still?" *Shut up*, I told myself.

"Turn." The famous dancer scanned me. "I see."

There was a silence. Dizzy, I came to a stop.

"Too short," Miss Ruth said. "Wrong body type."

"I can be taller." I straightened my shoulders.

"You have no elevation. Your height is...?"

"Five foot, two inches, but I have a spring—"

"And, Miss Grisholm, your age would be...?"

"Twenty-two. Late to start, I know, but—"

"Too old. Most of our girls start out as children."

"I'll work extra hours to make up for that and—"

"Too plain. Too dark. No curls." Ruth sighed.

"Wait outside," Louis told me. "They'll call you."

Ted came in and shot me one swift and searing glance. A dancer himself, his auburn hair glowed, backlit, like a halo. His smile, however, was devilish. He turned from me to his wife and frowned. I went to stand out in the hall. From there, without shame, I eavesdropped on the couple's discussion of their newest applicant.

"Oh that girl, Ted, she's a disaster."

"Wait. I need an Asian maiden. She'd do."

"*Too ugly*. Maybe she could play a boy."

"Good. Ruthie, tell her she gets a small part."

I had made it into Denishawn. As a boy.

~~~

"You have to go where you're called," I told Louis later. I knew where I was meant to be. My father had led me here and given me his blessing. And now I would just have to prove myself, even though I felt as if I'd just staggered away from a near-fatal car wreck.

Miss Ruth's hard words would come back to me, I knew. They sounded like echoes of my worst childhood moments. Ahead of me lay the next humiliation: Binding my breasts so I could resemble a boy. After that, though, I would work and watch and grow into my destined role. Now I lifted my head, squared my shoulders, and walked past Louis, still at the piano.

For me, he banged out "Happy Birthday." In a way, that's what it was.

For a year, he noticed how quickly I gained confidence and mastery of my body's movements. Denishawn drew on classical ballet as well as Eastern forms of dance. Miss Ruth showed how movement could be spiritually expressive — Ted taught me technique. Without complaint, I danced in the back row of the chorus, on the end, where I could be ignored.

In a sari, with a red dot on my forehead, there I was, a direct descendent of the Mayflower Pilgrims. My black hair and dark eyes led Ted Shawn to cast me only in exotic roles: Egyptian. Spanish. Aztec. Indian. Again, always placed on the end of that last row of the chorus. If anyone might watch — and I knew Louis did — he would see a girl dancing for the love of it, the thrill of it, the sense of a good wind blowing through body to soul.

Maybe Denishawn expected me to get discouraged and drop out. *Probably,* I suspected. *Too bad for them.* This only strengthened my resolve to stay. *I'll teach myself,* I decided. All of my free time went into my self-imposed assignments. With great care, I studied the senior students as they danced.

Soon I could discern "good" from "gifted" and I focused on the gifted students. Then, long after bedtime, I practiced everything I'd seen until I got it right. *My God,* I wanted to shout one evening. I *can memorize a dance from watching it one time.* And then a wave of sadness swept me. There was no one I could tell.

Only Louis seemed to notice me then. He alone watched me stretch and step and whirl through the dim studio, night after night. Toward the end of my first year at Denishawn, Louis told me I had finally made an impression. Even Ted Shawn saluted my passion for the dance. Dedication was mentioned, along with determination. But it was the passion and intensity that won him over.

Now Ted was laying out a new ballet for the chorus. He outlined a Spanish theme crossed with a North African motif. A "mishmash," he called it — but he knew the dance would make "good theatre." Good theatre equaled good box-office, as important as good art. And so Ted had the chorus doing his Hispanic-African arrangement when he saw me jump and leap in the last row. He called me out of line and drew me forward. "This," he put his finger on my collarbone, "is how it's done."

I flushed. The chorus dancers exchanged glances as they scattered at the rehearsal's end. Ted looked me over once again. His eyes scanned the long black hair, the exotic face, the dark eyes blazing out at him. Taking it all in, he shook his head.

"Too bad you don't know that Moorish solo."

"But I do," I told him. "I've watched every step."

"Kid, no one learns to dance by watching."

I took a breath, stepped back, and danced the solo.

I have to say, it was flawless.

"Perfect," Ted Shawn stared at me. "It's yours."

~~~

"Too short," "too old," "too ugly," I was a success.

Seranata Morasca would be my debut solo.

I went out to tell the peacocks. I had made no friends, only rivals, and there was no one else to tell. *I can learn a dance just from watching it,* I repeated to myself. I wished the peacocks could flutter in response. *I never knew I could do a thing like that.*

One of the birds darted in front of me, creating a splash of color in my path. The iridescent creature spread its fan-like tail. Even in the shade it shimmered. This was part of Miss Ruth's menagerie. If Ted had his way, he would have sneaked out in the night and wrung the neck of every peacock on the place.

"Puffed up with pride, all of you." He'd clap his hands to make the birds scatter. "You're not even graceful," Ted would call after them. "You move like hens in drag."

I had to ask Louis, "What is drag?"

He told me. Now I had another question.

"Do you think I'll turn into a peacock?"

"No!" He was stung. "Why ask me that?"

"I might disappoint you as Miss Ruth did me."

Louis laughed. "You couldn't be more different."

We walked together among the eucalyptus trees one evening. As the laughter faded, my face turned somber.

"What's wrong?" Louis asked. "Feeling guilty?"

"A little. Ruth enchanted me, now it's over."

"It happens," he said. "You won't be here forever."

We walked in silence, then went in to dinner.

The trees whispered like spies outside a palace.

~~~

"Turn and turn and turn. Again..."

Behind the ballet barre, tall mirrors flash.

"Spine straight. Breathe. *One* and two...."

Crack of flexing knees; crack of arching backs.

Up-tempo now: rehearsal for tonight. The show featured an unknown dancer's first solo. Louis congratulated me; Miss Ruth said nothing.

I knew I'd earned this solo. For a year I'd worked myself almost beyond human endurance. And as it happened, I'd won my featured part at the last minute: a fluke, a risk, a gamble. Denishawn kept drawing in fine students from all over America. Competition was intense for every single solo.

"You danced out of the chorus," Louis said.

"Well, it only took me thirteen months."

Another solo soon followed: A Moorish dance with Gypsy undertones, it suited my coloring. But it did more. It showcased my technique, developing by then. My left side-kick. My angular motions, my power to turn and turn. It was more than crowd-pleasing "good theatre," Louis told me later. "That was actually art."

To celebrate, he took me to a Chinese restaurant nearby. There I sat, ankles crossed, in a red leatherette booth, under clanging wind-chimes. They drew my eyes but I drew Louis's. I looked up, then down. My fortune cookie trembled in my hands. This was the first one I had ever seen.

This was the first man, since my father, who had ever taken me out to a restaurant. Nervous, I popped the whole cookie into my mouth and crunched it down in one go — paper, fortune, all. Louis was too polite to mention my blunder at the time. Later, he never let me forget it.

"How did you feel?" He asked about my solo.

"Like a horse." I saw his reaction and laughed.

He paused, trying to take this in. "A...horse?"

"Charged with power, hot to start."

"I see." He understood. "And once you start?"

"First you breathe. Everything starts there. Then you hear the breathing of the audience. You feel them out there, and something inside you connects with them. This...power, it runs through you to them but you're the one who opens the channel." My face felt hot. "This energy comes through us in different ways, I think. I'm talking too much."

"Are you ever pleased?" He studied me.

"I don't think artists ever feel that...do you?"

"Pleasure doesn't matter, really, I guess."

"I know!" My words tumbled out in another rush. "There's something else that makes you want to create. To move. To go farther..." I trailed off, abruptly embarrassed. I hadn't spoken that many words in an entire year.

~~~

Xochitl.

I never could pronounce the title of my next solo. This would be a new ballet-drama Ted designed for me. I was cast as a Toltec Indian maiden — what else? — whirling and pummeling my partner: a lustful emperor who was making unwanted "advances" on the heroine.' Read "advances" as rape.

The maiden was coached to be ferocious; I wonder if Ted lived to regret his fierce choreography. "Let her rip," he told me. "Give me hell, I can take it." I fought him off with such fury I left marks on his bare chest. Once I even grazed his face. Ted had underestimated the power and the passion of this woman-child in his arms.

The audiences loved to watch this contest of strength — *Xochitl* had the appeal of David and

Goliath. This time, though, David was a woman, strong enough to triumph over the giant. It was amazing that this dance had such appeal in 1922, but *Xochitl* earned standing ovations and did "good box-office." Receipts were as important as ovations. This was a business, Ted reminded me, as well as art.

At the time, Denishawn was more than the premiere school of American modern dance. It also had the premiere dance company in the United States. I was a key member of the company by 1921 — a principal soloist, a role unheard-of for such a diminutive dancer. I kept to myself but I knew some of the other girls resented me and called my "Miss Prim."

They were classic All-American types: blonde curls, light eyes, long legs like my younger sisters. Ironic that my maternal lineage was more "American" than anyone's. I was still typecast as the exotic foreigner at Denishawn. I even portrayed the Egyptian goddess, Isis, as well as Cleopatra. But I was no competition for the blondes.

Even so, my prowess irked a clique of "cookie cutter cuties" — a term coined by Louis. The leader of this clique was Liz, a long-stemmed blonde, not distinctive, but once Ted's favorite. "Watch out for her," Louis warned. "No gazelle, that one, but she has 'The Look' Ted likes. And her tongue can draw blood."

"Ted said I was his golden girl," Liz told me.

"Then I guess you are." I spoke with care.

"He says you have 'animal magnetism.' "

"Whatever that is." I shrugged it off.

~~~

One thirsty August afternoon, I went with Liz and four other dancers to splurge on sodas at a drugstore. I happened to be laughing as I came up to the soda counter. My laugh was low and husky; under strong lights, Louis said, my hair shone like a panther's.

Liz placed the orders for everyone, gave the clerk a dollar and asked for change. The clerk returned the change — to *me*. There was a sudden silence. Our chocolate sodas were consumed without a word. As we left the store, Liz broke into tears. Turning on me, she burst out:

"It's not fair — not fair at all."

"What's not fair?" I stared at Liz.

"I'm the *blonde* — but you're the *bombshell.*"

I sighed. "You'll never forgive me, either."

"How'd you know what I was thinking?"

"Your face. Your tears. You're transparent."

"And you're a witch, Miss Martha, that's what."

"Well, I hope no Kansas farm house falls on me."

"I hope it does — someday it will," Liz sobbed.

"You don't mean that," my voice was quiet.

Such an event seemed highly unlikely then.

~~~

Meanwhile, I went on tour with Denishawn.

Cities. Towns. Theatres. Civic centers. Opera houses. Grange halls. Opera houses, large and small, with the greatest dance company in the entire country. I learned about tipping porters, making costumes, making up my face. Louis used to watch this daring procedure with a mix of horror and fascination. "Women are amazing creatures," he would say.

I made everything into a ritual: Even the delicate art of beading lashes. First I lit a candle. Then, with ceremony, I blew out the match. The next step was to hold a stick of black wax in the flame until it softened just enough. The wax was stroked onto the eyelashes with a brush and under stage lights, how those lashes gleamed. I learned all this from reading an interview with Sarah Bernhardt.

Once, the tour stopped in Chicago and Louis, busy with rehearsals, sent me to the Museum of Fine Arts. Louis had exacted a promise from me. I must find a certain floor, a certain room, a certain painting, and when I saw it, I would understand this mission. I followed Louis's written instructions and came to an abrupt halt before an abstract painting by a Russian artist, Wassily Kandinsky.

The canvas, large and rectangular, was an electric blue. On the right side there was a vertical red slash that seemed to jump from the blue field. I stood there a long time. "Oh God," I whispered finally, my eyes on the Kandinsky. "I must thank Louis. That's *exactly* how I feel when I dance".

~~~

A wild beautiful creature.

Maybe from another world.

But very, very wild.

That's what I want to be.

I was confiding to Louis, late at night.

Rattling train, wailing engine; summer rain.

I *couldn't do anything I didn't feel.*

A dance dominates me completely.

I lose sense of anything else.

Another train rocked me through the night.

No idea where I was or where I'd been.

Too tired to care. Too jazzed up to sleep.

Twenty-one numbers a show.

Three shows a day, every day. ˙

Four solos for me in every show.

You could say I paid my dues.

Ted appointed me to manage one of Denishawn's touring companies. Suddenly, my work tripled and I took it all quite seriously — too seriously, some said; I knew. I felt both pride and panic about my new responsibilities. There were so many things to remember: The train tickets here. The hotel reservations there. The paychecks in my brassiere. The costumes inventoried every night. The beautiful wild thing had a good head for business. As long as everything was in its place. On time. Under tight control. Mine.

Sometimes the traveling chorus longed to strangle Martha-the-Manager. Still, I think I made a fairly good ballet mistress — meaning tough and inventive. To keep the show from going slack, I took the dancers by surprise, changing easy steps to harder ones. It worked. The troupe never lapsed into a mechanical routine. But dancing, directing, and managing a tour was a lot to put on one young woman. I was starting to show signs of strain.

~~~

Iowa City. I was a bit full of myself by then. In its small theatre, I chose to change the program. Back-stage, from the theatre pay-phone, I called Ted. Long distance, mind you, daring to reverse the charges.

"I'm adding a number to the show," I told him.

"You don't do programming," Ted shouted. "I do."

"I want that dance, damn it,"I shouted back.

"Don't be a bitch," he yelled. "I said 'No.' "

"What did you call me?" I was screaming.

"Bitch." Ted exploded. "Don't ring me again."

"I won't." I felt a flame of rage spiraling through me, far beyond my control. With both hands I lunged at the theatre's wall and ripped the phone out, letting it crash to the floor.

All I felt was my own fury; I didn't notice the wide eyes and frightened faces of the girls in my company. I didn't think about their feelings or morale. They stood staring from me to the hole in the wall back-stage. Without a word, Louis lifted the phone from the floor and stashed it out of sight. I cleared my throat and issued my next directive:

"Run-through in twenty minutes. Hurry up."

~~~

The tour had a grand finale at Grauman's Theatre in Los Angeles; not just any hall but a million dollar palace. Denishawn presented four shows a day to a packed house. The audiences leapt to their feet after every performance. Ted and I were remorseful about our argument and, in time, exchanged apologies.

Even so, things were never quite the way they were. The next time Ted's temper clashed with mine, he yelled at me from a taxi and shut the window so hard the glass cracked. We certainly knew how to set each other off.

Again, there was a period of recrimination, then remorse, then reconciliation. Until the next encounter, I knew. Louis wondered how long I would stick it out at Denishawn. He made a bet with me, giving me two weeks. When he heard of Ted's new plan for raising money, Louis changed his estimate to six days — at the most. This time he was right, almost to the hour.

On the crucial day, he was there with Ted and me at a low-priced coffee shop downtown. Its name was Harry's Kitchen but everyone referred to the place as "Harakiri." It was the kind of establishment where patrons routinely wiped the forks and knives with clean handkerchiefs. The best part of the menu were the prices. Lunch for me was always the same: Coffee, dark as motor oil, accompanied by a bacon-lettuce-and-tomato-sandwich. Even there at Harakiri, I could not afford to add the bacon.

Looking back, I thought the dive's name was a sign; perhaps a warning. Something ominous was on Ted's mind, I sensed, as I took a seat at the small table. Ted studied the salt shaker and the ketchup bottle as he worked up to his announcement. He lifted his smudged water glass in a mock toast and then began his speech.

Denishawn was desperate to raise more funds, Ted confided. Wouldn't it be a clever move if I offered lessons to sales girls in department stores? Not real dance; posture and deportment, that sort of thing. Of course the stores would pay Denishawn for every session, with a small "cut" for me. The "service" could branch out to several stores....

I stared at Ted as if he'd lost his mind.

"You're kidding, no?" Louis asked him. Twice.

"I'm a dancer," I snapped. "Not a 'demonstrator.' "

"Oh. You're Pavlova, right?" His voice rose.

"I'm an artist, damn it." My voice was rising, too.

"Don't use that goddamn cliche on me, Miss G."

"I won't compromise. You said *you* never would."

"I *have*," Ted yelled. "That's how you got a solo."

I leapt up, yanked the cloth off the table, and stood there shaking before I walked out. The sudden crash of crockery drew waiters on the run. Diners jumped in their seats. Stepping over three smashed plates, the restaurant's owner appeared. A heavy man with a florid face, he seemed shaken. Perspiration seeped through his shirt; he mopped his balding head. He was silent for a moment.

"Something wrong with the food?" he asked finally.

~~~

The next day, I was on the train to New York City. John Murray Anderson, producer of *The Greenwich Village Follies,* had seen me perform on tour. Impressed, he had offered me a job at the perfect moment — just before the lunch at "Harakiri." The pay was irresistible: Three hundred and fifty dollars a week. A fortune, in those days, to me.

I needed the money, I told Louis. My mother and sisters were struggling with bills in Santa Barbara. He watched me for a moment. "Were you trying to get Ted to fire you?" he asked.

I gave him an enigmatic smile. In any case, we all knew this much: I had squeezed what juice there was from Denishawn. It was time to move on, learn more, and get more exposure.

If Mr. Anderson heard any bad reports from Ted or Ruth, the Broadway producer would ignore them. He knew quality when he saw it and he hated backstage gossip. This was a good chance for me to make new contacts, learn more, and reach the artistic center of American dance.

Of course, John Murray Anderson's *Follies* were hardly "high art." Or "art" in any form. This was clear to me from the beginning. Mr. Anderson never pretended otherwise. He was getting me to New York, paying me, and giving me the pleasure of competing with Ziegfield's rival company. I was heading East to Gotham, everybody's promised land.

■

CHAPTER FOUR

In the Twenties, if a city in America could equal Prince Charming, New York had the shining armor.

"The war to end all wars" was past. Skyscrapers thrust upwards as their windows formed towering grids. Horns called; sirens sang, traffic hummed. Vendors' voices lifted, hawking hotdogs and hot chestnuts, fresh ice as in uncut blocks, and fresh ice as in uncut diamonds. For me, it all came together as one hell of an urban concerto.

Hemlines rose. Bobbed hair swung. Maids laden with packages trailed their mistresses along Fifth Avenue. Tiffany's windows showcased giant emeralds. Salons sizzled with the Charleston and clubs jumped with "juice" and jive. Standing in the April dawn, I watched Manhattan's skyline turn from copper to gold.

I raised my window higher and leaned out. In seconds, I smelled wet streets, waffles, curry, cigarettes, gardenias, gasoline — and I knew there was no other place for me. I was living in a tiny one-room walk-up on the fifth floor of a tenement in the East Forties. I had a cot, a bureau, a table, an ice box, and a fire-escape.

I also had infinite energy and insomnia. Manhattan seemed to be as sleepless as I was. I went out on my fire escape at all hours of the night to watch the city changing. And it always was. I thought of my perch as a balcony and my place as the Ritz, and that year, for me, it was.

I loved to watch the morning light finger the tall buildings. In that crack between night and day, I felt a slight pause in the city's pulse. There was something intimate about that moment, that view of Manhattan waking, waiting, winding up to pitch out a new day. The pulse became a throb; I could hear it escalating hour by hour — instant by instant.

Jazz was just around the corner. Tin Pan Alley's music filled the air. So did new names: O'Neil, Gershwin, O'Keefe, Stravinsky. Gin, illegal at the time, was everywhere. Money, too, it seemed. Boys bore armfuls of roses to penthouse doors. Ladies dropped thousands for bugle-beaded gowns. Gentlemen bought banks of box seats with crisp hundred dollar bills. Big time gamblers bet big bucks. And won. Like the Brooklyn Bridge, still new and strung with lights, the stock market defied the impossible.

Confident, optimistic, rich, the city soared into the future. And I was at its center — Times Square, light as day at midnight, flashing its brilliant signs of promise. "Home," to me, was the Winter Garden Theatre, as it was to *The Follies*: a place decorated like an emperor's palace and hung with elaborate chandeliers.

Backstage was a bit less plush but I hardly noticed. Outside the theatre's stage door, Manhattan waited for me. I walked as many blocks as I could, trying to absorb everything around me. Here was a city as restless and intense as I was, as edgy and strong-willed, as passionate about the arts and artists.

Even in the so-called "naughty" sections, where naked ladies danced and pornography was peddled, I felt the beat of life. How delicious for a sixth generation descendent of the Puritan Miles Standish. Even amid the garbage and the glitz, I found small gifts. A program from a Broadway play. A dropped orchid; a silver dollar. Once, atop a trash bin, a battered hat with one silk rose. Under it, a broken champagne flute. Every corner, I thought, had a story and in its own way, a touch of class.

~~~

A class act.

That was me, in the eyes of my producer.

Presenting "exotic dances" in the Denishawn style, attired in stark black or white, I was to be the gloss, the ace, the artist in the place and the show girls set me off. They wore glittering G-strings, sequined brassieres and huge feathered arrangements, taller than fruit-baskets, on their heads. Their spangled high heels clicked, their painted lips formed the most perfect pouts. Somehow, between the feathers and the footwear, their curves could gyrate. And did. I gave them all a lot of credit just for walking a straight line and staying upright.

As a Denishawn refugee, I made quite a contrast with the chorines. I was barefoot and bare-headed — but between my head and feet I was fully clothed. In my plain long skirts I might have been a Quaker caught at a carnival. Without plumes and heels, I looked so short, I seemed to be from another race.

In that setting, without glitter, I was totally devoid of glamour. I did not chew sensen; I did not smoke; I did not drink. "What *do* you do?" the show-girls sometimes asked with a wink of beaded lashes. One of them stopped me in the dressing room. "Mormon, right?" the showgirl asked.

It was a simple matter of economics, I tried to explain. I could not afford such pleasures as sen-sen or a chocolate bar more than once a month. I sent half my paychecks home each week. Even so, I did not feel at all deprived nor was I ever lonely. The city itself was my companion of choice. That first season with the *Follies,* I lived with the radiance of a girl in love. And so I was. Manhattan had bewitched me, obsessed me and enthralled me, even though I was consumed with work.

The chorines sashayed on stage for a lineup of high kicks, nine numbers for each performance. I had four solos every show, eight shows a week, every week, for twenty-four months. Now and then, I'd get tired and try out for other jobs. That meant giving up a day off to duck into a dive where a man with a cigar and red suspenders hollered, "Next!" The hopeful girls sat on folding chairs, waiting to audition.

"You," a producer would call. "Blondie."

"Yes, sir." The girl would stand and turn.

"You're the type. Curls and curves, ha-ha."

"Yes, sir." The girls always said. "Ha-ha."

"Where ya from?" That dreaded question.

I had an Irish friend, a dancer named Annie Moore; we sometimes auditioned together. Annie's last name was always mispronounced as "More" — often prompting a producer's off-color remarks. She was not ashamed of her roots but she needed work, and at that time, many employers still advertized jobs under one condition. *"No Irish need apply."*

"She's from Cheyenne, Wyoming," I always intervened when the question about origins arose in an audition. As an Easterner, I knew a cigar-chomping New York producer was not likely to chat about

Wyoming. Anyway, I never ran into a Manhattan impresario who had gone to high school in Cheyenne. Annie was always spared further questioning about her background — and kept on getting jobs.

"You." A producer would call me. "Blackie."

"My name is Martha," I would answer back.

"She's 'the nice one,' you're 'the sassy one,' right?"

"Find out." I would look right at the producer.

"Dark hair, dark eyes like...like who, for instance?"

"Try Cleopatra." A slow smile. "For starters."

"Don't say you're from Egypt. Can you dance?"

"Like the wind," I always said. "Watch me."

The producers stared at what I could do.

"We'll call *you*," I'd say as I left the premises.

"That's my line," the producer would shout.

~~~

Usually, I did get those call-backs, but in the end I stuck with the *Follies*. The pay was just too sweet and I needed it. My family was still struggling; more money had to go to their way. Practicality, not principle, turned me into a vegetarian. I could not afford to buy meat or poultry. I didn't have a working oven, anyway.

I stored light bulbs in that extra space along with a pair of ancient galoshes. I tried to hide such facts when I made my weekly calls to Santa Barbara. The pay phone at the corner drug store was my station every Sunday afternoon at six, when the rates went down.

"You have a laundress?" My sister Geordie asked.

"The best. Thorough." And I was, it was true.

"And you eat right?" Geordie sounded suspicious.

"You bet. Lots of fresh greens, very healthy."

"No meat? You used to make a mean pot roast."

"Darn it, gotta go, my coins are running out."

"Martha? Are you telling us the truth?"

"How can you ask? Would I lie to you?"

A pause. "Yes," Geordie whispered. "Yes."

"Time's up, operator's cutting in, bye for now."

The laundry was done in my bathroom sink with *Ivory "It Floats" Soap*. I was a whiz at ironing, spread across the table. At Christmastime, I did double duty, wrapping gifts at a friend's bookstore. I didn't make enough money to buy face cream but I was young enough — and rebellious enough — to relish my notion of Bohemian style.

I had never expected New York life to be easy. It was worth the sacrifices just to be there, even when the *Follies*' glamour faded during my second year there. I could never pinpoint just when, exactly, or just why this happened. The ever-present sequins from the shows seemed to symbolize the "why" if not the "when."

Silver, gold, and sometimes red, sequins were always floating around backstage and onstage at *The Follies*. Sequins fell off costumes, props, and scenery, and hung in the air, giving it a tawdry twinkle. Sequins stuck to my hair, my skin, my eyelashes, my feet; sequins even wafted into my brassieres.

"We're star-spangled banners," I told Annie.

"But we can't afford the firecrackers to go with them."

"We should *be* the firecrackers," I sighed.

"With cash," Annie said. "Christmas is coming."

The only gifts we could afford on Christmas Eve were pencilled notes. Each note held a list of promises to be paid in kind within a certain amount of time — and we took each item seriously. With proper formality, Annie and I took turns reading out our printed vows.

I will iron all your undies for a month.

I will clean your windows with The Times.

I will sprinkle Holy Water on your bed.

I will make an omelette for your birthday.

I will SELL MY BODY to afford the eggs.

"Martha! I thought we were being serious."

I will dance naked for ten bucks in cash.

"God, you're cheap, I'd do it for twenty."

I will send photos of you to your priest.

I will send photos of you to your mother....

On it went, under a pint-sized poinsettia, standing in for a real tree. We went to a crowded Midnight Mass at St. Patrick's Cathedral, known to us, true New Yorkers now, simply as St. Pat's. The next day we had a two-course Christmas Dinner as guests of the Salvation Army. Together, we fended off advances made by men "down on their luck."

"Cheers," an old sailor grinned. "Wanna fuck?"

I flashed him one of my most electric looks.

"I'm Santa, where's your chimney?" He persisted.

Still eating her pie, Annie kicked him in the shins.

"That should do it," she watched the pest exit.

The other men stayed clear of us after that and, in relative peace, we consumed every scrap of food on our plates, from lumpy mashed potatoes to gluey apple pie. We even broke our strict vegetarian resolve and ate the bit of turkey lurking underneath the gravy. After all, it didn't cost a cent. And once we'd cleaned our plates we had no complaints at all.

"Was that real turkey?" Annie wondered.

"Could have been horsemeat drowned in gravy."

"Oh my! You're teasing me. Aren't you? Was it?"

"Don't ask," I said. "You'll know if you whinny."

"Stop it." Annie laughed. "You're terrible."

"So I've been told, a bad seed. Happy Christmas."

~~~

In those days, I didn't feel a moment of self-pity, only pride in how well I was managing. On New Years Eve, Annie and I toasted each other with boot-legged champagne, sent over by Louis Horst. He had recently moved to New York after a trip to Europe. Exciting things were happening there in the arts, he wrote: "We have to talk soon. A new year's coming, you must have a new life to go with it."

On New Years Day, Annie and I exchanged written resolutions on fresh sheets of paper. Actually, they were the paper doilies from the Salvation Army dinner. Once again, scripted in pencil, our resolves were remarkably similar: *Get a new job, a new flat, a new toilet plunger, a second-hand wrench.*

No requests for anything impractical. No resolves to get a man. Not in writing, anyway. Life was tiring enough without the added complications of romance. We tucked our lists away and went down to the Winter Garden Theatre to get dressed for the holiday shows.

Always weary, often hungry, I wondered if I was wrecking my body before I ever got to do serious dance. I felt this in my very sinews: my destiny did not lie with the *Follies. I'm making do,* I told myself, *but I'm not making art.* I woke up trembling at this recurring thought: *I have turned into a 'hoofer,' not a dancer.*

I grew thinner, paced at night, hung onto the bathroom sink to do plies. Finally, it was not so hard to leave the Winter Garden Theatre, after all. Annie turned to waiting tables at the Schrafft's restaurant chain. I turned to teaching dance to regain my artistic mood and go on earning money. Entirely self-support-ing, I found myself maintaining a delicate balance — without an undergirding net.

Three times a week I traveled by train to the Eastman School of Music in Rochester, New York — 700 miles round-trip. Then I would rush back to the city and The Anderson-Milton School of Theatre Arts. *How can I do all this*, I asked myself. *Is this crazy?* I remembered Lizzie's steady labors and I kept going.

Now I watched my students closely, seeking out a core group for the company I hoped to found. In between I worked on my own dance movements, trying to break through to something I'd not seen before. Louis brought me out, I knew, helping me to shed needless remnants of Denishawn's style. No more Aztec dances, no more *Zochitl* imitations. "No more goddesses!" Louis shouted. "For Chrissake, move on."

I found three gifted students from Eastman. Louis felt I could put on a small show together with them. It took six months of preparation, stretching stamina and talent as never before. Louis nagged and needled, urging me on. He told me a new age had arrived in every facet of the arts. I had to step out — now.

Now. I repeated that like a magic word, a charm, a reminder to myself. *Now.* Sometimes I fell into bed, exhausted from two jobs and the push toward a new show. Other nights I walked the floors, wondering if I was throwing my young years away for nothing.

At last, the troupe got together and pooled its meager funds. Louis made an estimate: nineteen dollars altogether. I had to borrow money. Big money. So much money my hand shook as I held the bank note. "One grand," Louis said, as if he handled such sums every day. Then he put me in a taxi, got in beside me, and off we went off to rent a theatre for one night.

"A taxi?" I protested at the expense.

"What the hell," Louis shrugged. "Damage done"

"Looks that way." I elbowed him. "You stoic."

I soon became stoic, too, hopeful and stubborn, as the show took shape. "We have to gamble," I told my infant company. "We have to put ourselves out there to be judged on Broadway or always wonder about it."

I realized why Louis felt a sense of urgency. If I failed to take this risk now, I might lose my nerve and timing. *And* my youth. I had chosen a profession with a built-in limit to its life-span. Did I want to go on dancing for myself and for my friends at parties? All I had to do was ask the question and I was moving forward once again. The weeks were passing fast.

~~~

Show time.

Suddenly, it was here.

There was a frantic rush to be ready — everyone gathering together to sew the costumes I had designed. One sweet straw-haired man hanging lights for five dollars. Louis renting an upright piano for the eighteen numbers on the program. These were short dances I had created on trains, on buses, on the floor, in bed. I tried each one myself and felt a fleeting flush of excitement.

And then I looked up at the sky. Like white cinders, flakes of snow were falling on my upturned face. How could this be — on April 24th? Suddenly, I remembered: on this date I had first seen "the goddess" at the Mason Opera House in Los Angeles. A sign. An omen. That was all the reminder I needed on that night. The snow came down; the lights went on, the curtain rose.

~~~

My first presentation had a Denishawn flavoring: I felt embarrassed by one title in particular: *"The Three Gopi Maidens."* In other dances, I broke free of old patterns and began to show flashes of my future style. And, to my amazement, "Martha Graham and Dance Group" filled the house with enough patrons to pay off my loan and the theatre.

The critics came and filed polite reviews, with phrases like "pretty and undisturbing," and "exotically graceful." I was just relieved I'd paid my debt, but had no illusions about my audience. "They came," I said, "because I was such a curiosity — a woman who could do her own work."

Later, I looked back on that night with amusement and embarrassment. Even so, I'd won my gamble. I had been reviewed. I had filled a theatre. I had made a start — and cracked open a door for myself on the

Great White Way. "It was that," I had to agree. "Snow in April."

Now I knew there would be a next time and next time would be different. For one thing, I would read the weather reports. Meanwhile, I would keep developing new dances; I worked on these full-time for three months after the school term had ended. That year there were three significant events. In June, my lease was up. The *Follies* season ended.

I moved, alone, to a studio at Carnegie Hall.

"Don't be shocked by my place," I warned Louis.

Long and narrow, wider at one end, my single room had a chilling shape: it looked like an enlarged version of Dracula's casket. I called it "The Coffin," but all the same, I was thrilled about the flat's location.

Looking out on West 57th Street, I was living at the center of a legend: The country's fabled "cathedral to the performing arts." Carnegie Hall and Carnegie Tower have always been artistic honeycombs, filled with odd-shaped studios and living quarters for coaches, students and performers — active, would-be, had-been, semi-retired.

You could hear trumpeters and sopranos doing scales, dancers doing tap, and disembodied voices doing Hamlet, Odets and O'Neil. Out loud. The place was a maze of rooms with crazy numbering. I was in Studio Number 801 — on the sixth floor. They were separated by four steps. No one understood this; no one cared.

"Isn't it exciting, Louis?" I was fizzy as a Coca Cola. "I'm lucky, I have a harpist above me, an actress below. She's an understudy for an understudy in *Twelfth Night.*"

"How can you think in here? How can you *sleep?*"

"Sarah Bernhardt sleeps in *her* coffin."

"Let's not go *that* artistic. Don't you want sun?"

"I want my own studio, Louis. Two students—"

"*Here?*" he roared. "You can't turn around."

"I'll move the cot into that alcove, eat out."

"All the rest for dance?" he sighed. "Is that a life?"

"It is." My eyes were serious. "The one I want."

"You make my flat look like a palace."

Shaking his head, Louis opened the door.

"Stravinsky tonight," I called after him.

"I'm in," he called over his shoulder.

~~~

I became the ghost of Carnegie Hall.

One of them, at least.

Shameless, ravenous, I kept sneaking off to watch the world's great talent in performance: Toscanini, Duse, Pavlova, Rachmaninoff. I had a way with the ushers, trading seats for free dance classes and free tickets for my first ballet. I never said exactly when it would premiere or exactly what it was. But three years later, when I finally did make it, I went back to Carnegie Hall and distributed those promised tickets.

I could not inhale enough of what went on the boards there. And I knew what I saw was honing my eye and tuning my ear for what worked in performance. A certain gesture from the great actress, Eleanora Duse, left me in tears. A particular sequence by Pavlova was unforgettable, even though I did not have a heart for the ballet. Rachmaninoff awed me, as did Prokofiev, Stravinsky and that great conductor, Arturo Toscanini. And I remembered ever word, every gesture, every chord.

I saw a different kind of show in ball games when I went to Ebbets Field with Louis, a Yankees fanatic. I came away from double-headers talking about torsos while Louis talked of scores. But for me, nothing could compare with the offerings of Carnegie Hall.

"Who was it last night?" Louis asked me once.

"Bernhardt. Divine. With or without her coffin."

"Who's next? Can you sneak me in, maybe?"

I nodded. "I go to everything. Your choice?"

"Anything," he sighed. "Absolutely anything."

I paused, thinking. I knew the schedules by heart. Even so I rifled through a wooden box I'd set up on a fruit crate till I found a program I wanted to share. The floor beneath my knees was bare, the window lacked for curtains. Facing north, my flat didn't get a flood of light. I was broke. And never had I been so flushed, so lit within.

"Louis, I'm getting away from Denishawn's style."

"Good. I see you stopped wearing the sari."

"Please don't say that word again. How mortifying. What a silly girl I was. But now I'm doing it, I'm feeling my way into a new kind of movement. The dancing gives me energy to keep on teaching."

"But where on earth do you find the time?" he asked.

"I dance late at night, sometimes...all night."

"Don't kill yourself for this, Martha."

"It's life. I want to do something really new."

"You won't burn yourself out, though?"

I laughed; my face glowed, my eyes were lit.

"Burn out? I'll catch fire here."

~~~

The witch lived on Carnegie's sixth floor.

That was my floor, where I had to share a communal bathroom down the hall. This was where I first encountered the old woman I thought of as "the witch." One morning I looked into the wavy mirror as I washed my hands and there beside me was an ancient face, slack-jawed, wrinkled, but made up carefully with a professional hand.

She had been a performer once — I could tell by the woman's pencilled brows, powdered nose and faintly rouged cheeks. The mouth was rouged as well and gave the appearance of a wilted rose. One gnarled hand came into the reflection to refresh the makeup. I tried not to stare but her eyes strayed. The old woman turned to me, still looking into the mirror.

"I am Madame Beauchamps," she said.

"Good morning." I tried to be mannerly.

"And you are...?" Madame's brows arched.

I gave my name and occupation.

"I was a dancer once," the witch told me.

"I must have seen your name on a program."

"I coach dancers when I'm up to it."

"Maybe you can give me a few pointers."

"Don't humor me, young lady. Good day."

The next time I met the witch was in the Automat, an inexpensive self-serve restaurant on Fifty-Seventh Street. Cheap food sat under streaked glass counters and a cylindrical machine turned in endless circles, displaying its pies. I was about to get one, a slice of lemon meringue, when a gnarled hand grabbed my wrist.

"That one's three days old," warned Madame.

I asked for the old woman's recommendation.

"The chocolate one is new. Take it. Sit by me."

We sat in silence, watching the pie machine turn.

"Remember me when you grow old, my dear."

"I will. Maybe you would coach me some?"

"I'll coach you. For a pie. And company."

~~~

Madame's square room was filled with plants and light and photographs. Filmy lingerie hung from a clothesline in the window as did mine. Madame quickly snatched down her "unmentionables." She spoke of her life as a dancer, from a penny arcade on Atlantic City's boardwalk to a soloist with a French Ballet company. And then she asked me to walk across her Persian rug. I obliged. Next Madame asked the me to walk with my eyes closed. Again, I obliged. "How was that?" I asked. "What did you see?"

"My dear, you may be a great dancer."

"You can tell by watching me walk?"

"I can. Do this with your little class."

"If you say so, Madame, I'll try."

"Never tell a soul I coached you, Martha."

"Why not? What's wrong about that?"

"Let them think it all sprang from you."

"I see." I had to smile. "Okay."

"I'm nobody. But you'll be somebody."

"You're a great lady, Madame."

The old woman's eyes were sad.

"Don't dance too long," she warned.

Of course I forgot that warning — old age seemed so distant to me then. But at my next class I asked my students to walk, one by one, as I watched with a new sharpness. Then I had them walk together in a line. I whispered to myself, "I'll be damned, she's right."

I said no more; the moment passed. From then on, though, I always auditioned dancers that same way. Each one walked alone across the studio floor under my scrutiny. This observation made it easier to narrow the field. People asked me what my secret was. I never told anyone about "the witch" at Carnegie Hall.

"I've got to do something new," I told Madame.

"How new?" She offered me a chocolate.

"Not Isadora's Duncan's modern style, too vague, too Greek for me." I hesitated. "You were trained in classical ballet. But I'm drawn another way."

"You said your sister taught you ballet?"

"I loved it." I sighed. "But I want more now. I want to dance modern themes. I want to dance what I feel. What I think of as a kind of inner landscape. Here." I tapped my head. "I need different movements to express it all. But I can't seem to find anyone who teaches them. Not the kind I see in my mind, my dreams, everywhere."

"Ever try to learn Chinese? No? I'm serious."

"You mean...learn a different dance vocabulary?"

"You're a quick study, Martha. But vocabulary isn't everything." Madame's eyes glinted. "There's grammar, syntax. And eventually, verse."

"Where can I learn that?" I waited.

"Listen to me, darling." The old woman's voice was quiet. "For centuries, we've heard ballet's 'language.' Denishawn's 'speech,' rooted in the East, is older still." She paused. "Martha, if you want a new dance 'language,' you'll have to invent your own. Quite an undertaking. Have another chocolate."

The light had shifted, slanting through the room. In the street below, traffic hummed. Newsboys, shouting, hawked the afternoon editions. Time had passed without my notice and now I rose to leave. "I've stayed too long. Thank you, Madame. You're more than generous. You're wise."

"Foolish. I've daunted you. Stay a bit."

"I'm working on something, Madame."

"In your mind? Or in action?"

"Both. I see this line of figures, all in black, like Puritans." I closed my eyes. "Hard faces, stiff bodies. Together, they oppose a single figure. One female in white. Long skirt. Very plain. Barefoot, hair loose down her back." I took down my long hair and stood up. "She chops the air and...turns like this...then this." Each movement was precise, strong, angular. "Now she faces the dark line before her. She steps forward, a kind of supplicant...."

Feet braced, Madame planted herself before me.

"Yes. Exactly. Simple. Now turn another way."

Madame blocked me. I took one deliberate step forward. Again I could not pass the figure standing in my path. This forced me into a step to the right. Movement answered movement and I sensed something had changed and somehow we were dancing.

In the dim flat, past the cot and hot plate, past the two old chairs, I went through one sequence, then another, wordless now. In my mind, I saw a line of rigid figures lunge at me, then in one swift pivot, turn their backs on me in scorn. Kneeling, I bent backwards, as if I might fall. Then I rose only to melt forward toward the floor once more.

Dusk, rising like water, filled the room. We'd been so engrossed, we had not thought to turn on a lamp. Still silent, we looked at each other: Two dancers, caught by darkness, pausing in a wedge of space high above midtown Manhattan. Madame was tired now; I could have danced for hours more, though I had no inkling this would lead to one of my ballets.

When *Heretic* premiered in New York City three years later, it was hailed as my first major work. *The New York Times* had sent its dance critic, John Martin, who hailed the piece as "strikingly original and glowing with vitality." I rushed out to buy as many newspapers as I could afford and carry back to my room.

There was also praise in the review for me. Bless John Martin, who could be quite stern at times. He called me a painter using movement instead of oils; I created something new out of nothing at all, and it was not only strong, it was lyrical as well. *Heretic*, for him, was a vindication of the movement starting to be known as "Modern Dance."

Visually dramatic in black and white, this new ballet was unlike anything that came before. Its choreography was stark and provocative. Not "pretty." For much of my life, I'd been "different," so at odds with conventional female behavior. Now I had dared to dance in public like a heretic. But this time, I drew applause.

I had started this ballet in the "Coffin Room" at Carnegie Hall — I don't know how I dared to perform it. I was a lone figure in white facing that black line I had imagined: hard-faced, puritanical, unsmiling. Their movements were almost geometric. I wanted them to seem like an unfeeling machine and as I watched them, I felt a chill. I think I made my point.

Like a Greek chorus, the line dancers moved as one. Each of their motions were rigid while the suppliant in white danced with fluid grace. The climax came with my newest movement: A spiral fall, spinning downwards to my knees, leaning backwards until one shoulder brushed the stage, daring to go off-balance for a just a moment.

I had trained myself to spiral upward once again, as I've done so many times since: a movement requiring control and strength and practice, practice, practice. In *Heretic*, however, I chose to end the ballet with the suppliant collapsing: a crumpled figure of defeat who could not rise. The curtain came down on that still white form, crushed at last, lying in a heap on the bare stage.

From the audience, I heard a gasp, then someone sobbing out loud in the theatre. And then the swell of applause. At the time, no one was aware of my childhood struggles, all bound up within this dance. *Your legs are too short for dancing.* I sensed this, though I did not know for certain. Art had to come from somewhere, I thought. *This child bears the taint of Original Sin.* And art could push back through its magic in the oldest struggle: light against dark.

Why can't you be more like your sisters? This first work, perhaps, was not a deliberate answer to earlier rejections. *Stop posing. What on earth gets into you?* I didn't know the answer on a conscious level. "That piece just had to come out," I told Louis." That was that." In the end, I supposed my answer lay within the ballet itself.

When I moved out of "The Coffin" to a larger flat in Greenwich Village, I told Madame we would never say "Goodbye." Of course Madame was in full agreement. We would only say *"Au revoir"* — "To seeing you again." I promised to visit soon but days turned into weeks and weeks into months. At last I took the bus uptown and went to Carnegie's sixth floor. I knocked on Madame's door. No answer. I knocked again, more forcefully. Under that pressure, the door, unlocked, swung open.

The room was bare. There was no sign that anyone had lived there and there was no one to ask. Had she been evicted? Had she simply moved? I hated to think of another alternative. I looked for Madame in the laundromat, the Automat, the bench we'd shared in

Central Park. The old woman had disappeared. Almost. But not quite.

Sometimes I thought I caught a glimpse of Madame in several theatres, sitting in the audience. One here, one there. But by the time I could reach her seat it would be empty. This would only happen during curtain calls: a flash of Madame's lit face, a smile, a glint in the eyes — and then it was gone.

I saw that flash at *Heretic's* premiere.

I would always look for it, I knew.

■

CHAPTER FIVE

The view from Hades isn't always bleak. Graced moments appear along with grieved and guilty ones. A welcome respite, these good segments. I see how much I took for granted.

Take a fall day in 1927. An ordinary day; or so it seemed at the time. There I was, flying down a narrow street, swinging with its twists and turns. The street widened then, opening before me, and I did the *hop-jump-hop* of an impish child, skipping my way down the cobblestones into the future.

I stood still for a moment, tilting my face toward the amber light of late afternoon. I passed cafes and cabarets, shops and brownstones, outdoor booksellers, the sketch-artists, the corner fiddler. Caught up in a sudden swirl of autumn leaves, I spiraled with them till a pair of poets applauded from the nearest outdoor café. My curtsy was deep and regal, my smile a flash, and then I lifted my lips as if to kiss the day, the sky, the sun before they faded away.

On the air, I smelled coffee and garlic, reefers and apples. I was precisely where I had hoped to be: Greenwich Village, NYC. *Almost home now.* My thoughts jumped ahead as I turned the corner onto West Tenth Street. In an old stone house, the color of city snow, my new flat waited on the sloping second floor — a grand spread of space to me after "The Coffin Room" at Carnegie Hall.

Here I had two rooms, the smaller one for sleep, the larger one for my dance studio. Fresh from Tin Pan Alley, a new song ran through my mind: *"If I didn't have a cent, I'd be rich as Rockefeller...."* The song-writer had it right, to my way of thinking. Rich was how I felt as I scanned my first real studio.

The smaller chamber was crammed with necessities: a dresser, a night stand, lamps, a bed, and next to it, a third-hand typewriter perched on a low table. The keys of this machine had lost their spring, their clatter, but they served me well enough. I felt compelled to record ideas whenever they surfaced, even in the night: stories, dreams, dance patterns, lines of verse I must not forget. I was a habitual scribbler, jotter, list-maker, though my notes made no sense to anyone but myself.

I preferred to keep it that way.

"Tap-tap-tap." Louis echoed the sounds that punctuated his sleep. "I think of it as rain on the roof, a soft

pattering, and I just turn over." He understood: those "three o'clock thoughts" might yield a new motif or sequence, even the germ of a ballet. "You never know," Louis gave a wiseman's nod. Often he made late-night notes on his music, reworking a piece or arranging reworks a new one. We flexed for each other's creative ferment, even when that led me to dance alone at night in the darkened studio.

This, the larger room, was almost bare. Crammed against its far wall was a galley kitchen, featuring a singed kettle, two thick diner mugs, and a tall jar of *Sanka* instant coffee, never full. No garlic strings hung above the tiny icebox; no pans perched on the two-burner stove.

I hid the kitchen with a curtain and turned my back on it. The rest of the studio seemed to offer an acre of empty space, dwarfing the babygrand piano, courtesy of Louis, and a shelf jammed with his prized books.

The studio had huge windows; these gave the place some gloss and seemed to deepen its space. Better still, they faced the front of the "White House," as I called it in a joking mood. Now, nearing home, I looked up and saw the lights were turned on in the flat; its window panes had taken on a shine. Louis, there ahead of me, must be reading one of his books or rifling through his sheet music.

I see Louis as he was then: portly, graying, rum-pled, head bent, turning pages, poring over volume after volume. Libraries were his *alma maters;* he had quit school early on, finding it a pretentious waste of time. Instead, he'd chosen to seek learning on his own terms and he'd studied alone, gleaning a broad knowledge of poetry, history and art.

"I think that's marvelous," I told him. "Marvelous! *Everyone* should learn that way." Louis Horst's heavy features spread into a smile so broad, it erased his jowls.

"Sometimes you make me feel like a prince in disguise. Heavy disguise." Louis gave one of his deep chuckles. "You can do that, you know. You're Circe, I think."

He and I were sitting together in Washington Square. Louis had given me a quarter and sent me to his bakery of choice for sweets: Danish pastries — apricot for me, apple for Louis. He was treating me to a rare banquet, "just for the hell of it," he'd said. Off and on, he surprised me in quirky ways; he knew I had lived on hard-boiled eggs, bruised apples, day-old bread and rolls aptly named "jaw-breakers."

Without making me feel indebted to him, Louis tried to punctuate my poverty with a bit of *gemütlich*: good times. That was an important notion to his immigrant parents, though Louis dared not speak a word of German during *The Great War*. People were no longer wary of him, a man so gifted, so gracious, he defied prejudice. He was a paternal presence to me, ten years his junior. He was my mentor, ally, coach and now, my lover.

"Turn right," he commanded me. I glanced at sunlight skidding down the stones of the famous Washington Arch, modeled on the L'Arc de Triomphe. "Turn left," Louis directed me then. I scanned a sun-splashed row of outdoor chess players, crouching over stone tables.

"Turn around," he commanded once more. The morning light was glowing on the Square's elegant brick houses, suffusing them in a brief rosy flush. "Where else could you find all this in one place?" Louis asked me.

"Paris?" I offered. "The City of Light?"

"Nowhere else," he boomed. "End of conversation."

I tried not to argue with Louis whenever he used that tone. My deference surprised me and, at first, as did my interest in this shambling man with the occasional grease spot on his tie. His suits never quite fit. His socks rarely matched. With my eye for simple elegance, I made, laundered, and pressed my own clothes. What a pair we made, I thought. All wrong together — and somehow, all right.

"How did you two meet?" we were often asked.

"Denishawn," we would always answer as one.

"Love at first sight? Dancer and the musician?"

"None of your damn business," Louis snarled.

~~~

An accomplished pianist, orchestrator, and *maestro*, Louis had come of age in California where his father was a trumpeter with the San Francisco Symphony Orchestra. Music perfumed the air of the

Horst home, where Louis had lessons in piano and violin. At the keyboard, the boy was a natural, and soon his father found him jobs with a variety of orchestras. In between, Louis played piano wherever there was work — movie theatres, clubs, casinos, even brothels.

Louis Horst soon had a reputation for talent, experience, and taste. Denishawn had grabbed him at a rare moment when he was between jobs. Fascinated by the confluence of dance and music, Louis had stayed on there, upgrading routine scores. By the time I'd arrived, Louis had made noticeable advances in his programming. "That's Debussy," I would whisper. "That was Strauss." And then I'd clap my hands, lifting them high.

Louis found me beautiful, defying stereotypes, and he felt the heat, the wild intensity I projected without realizing it. And yet I was virginal, with an air of vulnerability about me then. I didn't know which quality drew Louis to touch me the first time. I never knew exactly when that touch became a caress, and then a kiss, and then the slow unbuttoning of my blouse. To Louis I was that strange wild creature I had hoped to be:

A waif crossed with a wildcat.

And now he had made me his.

. ~~~

In my Greenwich Village flat, I had grown accustomed to the smell of his cigar smoke in the books, in the curtains, even in the fur of my three cats. Louis was there so much of the time, the neighbors assumed he lived with me. He did and he didn't, I told close friends when they asked. Louis kept his own flat two blocks from mine, but we spent most of our time together. I made a different schedule for us each day:

Morning coffee, morning class. Ferry rides and bus rides. Suppers mostly at the Automat or Horn & Hardhart self-serve cafeterias. Outings to Madison Square Garden and Yankee Stadium. I was as savvy as Louis, talking about "line drives" and "sliding into first;" and I loved baseball almost as much as he did. Fascinated by human movement, I saw grace in sports and theatre in that lit-up stadium.

If we didn't go to a game on weekends, we went to plays and concerts — always in the cheap seats. We strolled hand-in-hand through the Village, murmuring to each other in low voices. And, at times, the neighbors heard our raised voices, growing louder, sharper, uglier, behind the closed door of my flat. From time to time, the same subject surfaced: Louis had left a wife in San Francisco and stubbornly refused to get a divorce.

"Why why why?" I wailed; a plaintive sound.

"I won't discuss this again," Louis shouted.

"No kids, no love, no church—" I began.

"I said I won't go into it again. End of conversation."

A door would slam; he would storm into the hall.

Eventually, we would reunite and share supper.

Until the next time.

And there always was a next time.

The best I could do was defer it.

~~~

That October day, all I wanted was an agreeable meal, an amiable evening, an amorous night. I should have bought the sausages instead of the sunflowers. But the sunflowers had looked glorious to me; I could describe them no other way. In one hand I clasped five blooms, the last of the season, counted out precisely. I had not been able to afford a dozen — even half a dozen. Once again, I would have to borrow a dime from Louis for coffee, a nickel for the uptown bus the nest morning.

Even so, there had to be a touch of *gemütlich* to life. Louis had taught me that and surely he would understand. Flowers brought this quality right into my home. Sausages most certainly did not. Here the tawny burst of giant sunflowers would set off the blue burlap I had hung, floor to ceiling, on the apartment's dingy walls.

With these yellow blooms beside my bed, I would dream of touring Tuscany with Louis and my own dance company, newly formed. I could hammer one of those dreams into reality, at least.

~~~

Before touring anywhere, I knew, I must create that dance company. My technique was developing into a detailed program, starting with floor work — something unheard of at that time. I did not care if seated stretches and extensions were "done" or not. I rarely chose to defy gravity: a major goal of classical ballerinas and their choreographers.

"Don't just sit on the floor, root yourself there." I'd urge my classes to *use* gravity, claim it, work with it as a helpful element. To me, it was a great star covered with water and earth. Mother Earth. I moved about the studio. "Make your heels grip what's under them," I told my students. "Reach for the stars on grounded feet. Sway like rooted grass."

Then I sprang into the air as if a gust of wind had actually lifted me. This was one more way to compensate for my lack of "elevation," in dance terms. I realized how tiny I looked in the studio, barefoot, my long dark hair tied back, my white skirt floating to mid-calf. Onstage, though, I knew how to summon up a different appearance.

"I am Elizabeth Regina," I would sometimes tell myself in the wings as I moved out into the lights. On stage I always felt tall, thought tall, moved tall — was tall. As I did, I turned my mind to the great queens of history and myth; I had memorized their stories and their pictures. Even so, I myself was never quite sure how I conjured up their majesty.

"There *is* technique, very important, always, but there is *no formula*," I told my students. I worried about "my girls," young and mesmerized by my presence. *They must not be copies of me*, I wrote in my notebook. *We must burst into our own unique blaze. But with discipline, not relying on pure improvisation...they must care, must have passion....*

"*Curl* your torsos like a cat about to spring," I urged them on. "More. *More!* Be savage. You're a hunter, you want to pounce." I could hear the creak and crackle of stretching joints.

"*Thrust* your pelvis forward." I glanced about. "*Pelvis!* Yes, that's what I said. Don't pretend you don't have one. *Thrust. Again.* Passion. Dance from your core. I mean it. From your soul." Each girl did a pelvic thrust, trying not to flush or laugh at my use of a "forbidden" word.

"*Raise* your heads. Higher. Higher!" I tapped my students' backs. Recalling a note I'd typed for myself, I went on, "Be a pine tree." The girls struggled to obey. "Jane, are you a tree? Or a posy?" The redhead went from primrose to pine.

"*Extend* your necks. No no no. Not like that." I prowled the studio. "You are swans, stretching, stretching those long necks. Better. Yes. You can do so much more than you imagine."

I saw my students as a new set of younger sisters — kindred spirits this time, beautiful to me now, even when they were plastered with sweat, working in simple leotards, standing on bare feet. No ballet shoes, no constricting clothes; not here. No tutus, no togas, no exotic robes, either. Just the human body, which was glorious to me, finally unveiled.

"*Straighten UP.* Higher. Firmer. *Become a spear.*" I felt my energy go out into the class as the students stretched, bent, flexed, then stood again like spears. I knew they awaited my next words. I searched for the right ones. I wanted to do more than teach; I wanted to inspire.

"Now walk on an open diagonal across the floor."I remembered how Madame had taught me how much showed up in a student's walk — and in my own when Madame coached me. "Walk and walk and...."

"I can't just walk," a student said. "I mean, where am I going?"

"Move as if you're passing through a summer meadow. Wildflowers are bordering your path." That had a good ring to it when spoken out loud. "Now move into an all-out run."

I recalled my own anguished gallop through that frozen field, so long before, after my brother's death. "Think of grass beneath your feet. Move as if you're leaving pain behind you. Good."

It was time to push them harder now, I knew. Time for learning how to start a spiral fall: another movement I had worked out late one night. "We're going to use our spines a different way. Lean back. No no no. You're *not* a swooning maiden. *You are a tree bending in the wind.*"

They flinched and flexed their spines, careful to stay balanced. I wove my way throughout the room, my eyes keen, noting who was trying — and who was simply going through the motions.

"Now Ann." I paused before a student. "Your body says, 'Oh well, I'm a tree, who cares?' *You must care.* Understand? Again. And breathe."

Another long, listening pause. Too long now, too silent.

"I hear no breathing." I called, "Have we all died?"

From the piano, Louis gave a snort of laughter.

Time for what the girls call "The Torture," I reminded myself. I demonstrated once again. A gut-wrenching pull of stomach against spine. A deep bend at the waist. Slowly I released my breath. The class stared at me with awe — and dread. This hurt, I knew, at first.

"Now you. No groans, please. It's the same movement you get with a deep sob. Not bad. Again." I would not let up. "This time think of a deep laugh. Contract...release. Contract, release. Be brave. Once more...."

For twenty years, no mirrors lined the Graham studios — a rarity. The danger, I knew, was a dependence on the mirrors, until a dancer struggled to perform without her reflection. It was demanding to be a "Graham girl" but the students were proud of our rigorous "sisterhood."

~~~

"No, no, no!" Louis Horst barked at the class. I felt a surge of gratitude to him, although I knew he terrified some of the girls. Tough, strict, demanding, he made every dancer do a sequence until it was right. Nothing sloppy, vague or flighty was to be tolerated. I knew this from sessions with Louis at home.

"Toss that sequence in the trash," he snapped at Bess, a stunning blonde. "Start all over again. Tears won't help. Show me what you think you're doing. Do you have a clue?"

"I don't see what's wrong," Bess answered.

"That's perfectly apparent. I told you, 'Toss it out.'"

"But why?" Red-eyed, frantic, Bess pressed on.

"Because I said so. End of conversation."

A silence. Bess slammed out of the studio.

"What did I say?" Louis raised his palms.

"What didn't you say?" I used my driest tone.

"I watched my father practice eight hours a day before he made it into an orchestra." Louis turned to me, then to the class. "Do you think he's the only artist to have discipline? He puts some of you to shame."

"They make *me* proud," I flared up at Louis.

"They're not spun glass. And neither are you."

He was exacting, yes. Demanding, too. Accurate, always. And how I learned from him. We all did. It hurt, I knew. But we learned. By God, we learned.

Only I knew then how often Louis quietly paid a student's rent or loaned a dancer money. He cared about these girls more than they ever realized, even if some of them referred to him, in whispers, as "The Ogre." And I also knew he cared so much for me, he gave me the toughest treatment of all, forcing me to grow — in front of the whole class.

"What's that step for? You're mincing." He told me. "Mincing isn't good enough. You can do better than that, much better, and you know it."

"Nothing's good enough." I turned on him. "It's my own idea."

"Get a new one. I can't stand by and let you settle for mediocrity."

"*Mediocrity?*" My voice was rising. "I *beg* your pardon, Louis."

"I think you should. There, I made you mad, you've stopped mincing."

"*I do not mince.*" I yelled, "What do you want from me?"

"Your best. And more." He was quiet now. "Don't waste your gift."

"I certainly will not. It's you — quenching the spark, the flame."

"I want a *bonfire*. Use *all* your fuel, damn it."

"You're so smart," I scolded him. "Watch this sequence."

"Quit improvising!" He roared. "Don't dilute your talent!"

"That goes for us all," I turned to everyone. "Remember."

Amid the stretching and straining, contraction and release, there were lighter moments in the studio.

When I designed costumes, the company gathered together, each dancer sitting cross-legged on the floor. Bright swatches of material were spread out on our laps; needles flashed under the lights. There was chatter, there was laughter.

"There's a goddamned 'Sewing Bee' going on here," Louis snorted. "I'm leaving before the subject turns to cramps and *coitus interruptus.*"

"What's that, Louis?" A younger student asked.

"Tell them, Martha." Louis made a hasty exit.

All the girls looked at me; I was unperturbed.

"Useful term," I said. "You all should know it."

~~~

The studio hosted gatherings at Christmastime when every member of the company contributed cake and brownies, punch and fruit. And then there was the communal cleanup for the annual visit of my mother. Her fortunes had improved; her home in Santa Barbara was quite lovely; the Graham girls always wanted to make our studio impressive in its own way.

One year, preparations for "The Visitation" were left to the last minute. A bout of flu had knocked the studio off-schedule for a week. Now, everything took the form of a mad scramble. Quickly, dancers and students grabbed for cleansers, rags, paint brushes, and sponges. There were only twenty-four hours to get everything just right.

Working overtime, class and company tried to make our "home" glisten under the strong lights. Every inch of the studio was scrubbed and brightened, including the tiny bathroom and my desk. I asked a new student to touch up the faded toilet seat with fresh white paint. I mopped the floor myself. Someone polished the barre and Louis took care of the piano.

When Mother arrived later that day, everything looked *perfect*, I said. *Perfect.* Beer, punch, and home-made prune pie were served and Mother exclaimed over the studio. Then, excusing herself, she ducked into the bathroom. After five minutes, she had not emerged. The bathroom door was locked. Uneasy now, I glanced in its direction.

No one wanted to disturb a lady in such a private, possibly embarrassing situation. Another minute passed. Then, at long last, Mother's voice came through the bathroom door. As that voice rose, panic struck the studio. Listening, everybody seemed to freeze. The words from the bathroom grew into frantic cries for help.

"Unlock the door," I shouted. "I'm here."

"Oh my dear, I would, I would, but I simply can't."

"I'll call the janitor," I knew I'd gone white as salt.

"Oh no." Mother was pleading now. "No men!"

I forced the lock and the door swung open.

"Don't look!" Mother shrieked — too late.

Everyone gasped. There was my mother, stuck to the toilet seat with a thick coat of half-dried paint. The student responsible was already halfway down the stairs. No one dared to chuckle. Not then. Not the next week; not the next month.

A full year later, as the studio prepared for another Visitation, a sudden wave of helpless laughter swept the room. I stopped it with one electrifying look. I always referred to the previous year's incident as Mother's "holiday accident."

~~~

After my own holiday with Louis in New Mexico, I threw myself into a new creation: A major ballet, *Primitive Mysteries*. It was daring, I knew, and my most ambitious work, based on Spanish-Catholic ceremonies I had watched for hours in Santa Fe.

For me, this ballet was almost like the Mass itself, celebrated through my dance. I dreamed it, breathed it, moved through it in my mind. Even so, the concept did not clarify. Slowly, the work changed shape. At last, I saw *Mysteries* as a timeless ritual honoring a Madonna figure: the sacred female principle. Still, something was missing.

Struggling, I paced the floor at night and heard something in my own footsteps: a ritualized walk, but not a "pretty" one, took shape in my mind. I recalled the power of silent Catholic processions that I watched in New Mexico: a line of marching figures behind an elevated statue of the Virgin, stark, stiff, beautiful in white. I wanted to make this image even more power-ful. But how? For weeks, no answer came.

And then I heard a drumbeat in my mind, a sound that followed me from sleep into my waking moments. This was more than my own pulse, always my guide. Suddenly I knew where I had heard this drumbeat: in New Mexico, where I had watched Indians, in full regalia, presenting an ancient tribal dance. They stamped the ground, circling, passionate and worshipful.

I brooded over these conflicting images for weeks. Catholic. Primal. Christian. Pagan. Gradually I saw them merge, melt together, become one. In *Mysteries* I dared to infuse a Catholic processional with the power of Indian sacred ritual. It took me months to work out this opening procession, presented in silence so intense, the only sound was from the dancers' feet striking the stage. The tension built until the music started, lifting in a hymn of praise, followed by a deeper sacred silence. I knew this wasn't like any other ballet. It had to be done again, again; it had to be lived out, I thought, not only danced.

For a year I worked on *Sacred Mysteries* but never felt satisfied with it. *How to get what I see into movement?* I asked myself late at night. I was trying to synchronize myself with a holy heartbeat. No small task. Did I have the necessary talent? How far could I go — how much should I dare? With the class, I tried out sequence after sequence, trying to translate the sacred force into new steps, new gestures, all new choreography.

At every turn, something seemed to block me. The second part dealt with the Crucifixion and I didn't know how to express its agony. I wanted to be reverent; I wanted to be dramatic. Mary did not move at the foot of the Cross. How could I show the Virgin's anguish? I tried a new series of movements. No good. The ballet was stalled.

Nobody could get it right. I could not get it right. Louis could not get it right. Finally, frustrated with myself, I felt something boil over inside. What was wrong? "Miss Ruth's" wounding words come back to me. *Too old, too short, too ugly.* Why did I keep trying?

Maybe I had reached too high, too far beyond my own abilities. *Can't she see she's hopeless?* I tried to shut out those repeating words. It was impossible. *Hopeless hopeless hopeless.* I could not get this dance across, I never would. I had wasted everybody's time and energy. I was furious at them and at myself.

"Go away," I yelled at the class. "It's all wrong. A waste of time."

I slammed into my dressing room. In that small dark space I stood trembling, my back to the door. Again, old voices came to me.

Your legs are too short for ballet.

Why can't you be like your sisters?

Difficult, different, always trouble....

"Wait," Louis told the class. "It'll be okay."

Jerking the light cord, I saw a photo on my dressing table. My father's mild gaze seemed to study me. Did you think it would be easy? Even with your gifts? I could almost hear his mellow tone. *Think about the girls out there. Forget yourself for now.* I heard my own voice now: *Contract... release. Contract ...release.* I bent. Straightened up. Gulped air. And opened the dressing room door. I looked into fifteen pairs of staring eyes. "We'll start again," I said. "And *one...*" I started the count and pulled the class back into motion. "Attack this dance as 'Now.' "

They did; I did. Slowly it began to take new form.

~~~

Opening night. At last.

Primal Mysteries had made it to Broadway.

Still, I felt something terrible was about to happen to me, to us all, onstage.

I could see my loyal troupe — young, so very young — gathered in a theatre's wings. *Stretch, bend, flex.* The girls were silent and agitated, far beyond the usual pre-curtain jitters. This should have been a proud night for my handpicked dancers: "The Group," here to dance a Martha Graham World Premiere Ballet. I must not spoil it for them. But the work, I felt, was still not right. I said nothing and adjusted my skirt with trembling hands.

Panic spun through me and this time I knew I could not control it; I could not dodge this demon. Skidding like a child on an icy street, I felt I had to stop this ballet now or it would be a public disaster. I began to feel paralyzed, weak, sick to my stomach.

"It's not finished," I told Louis. "It won't work."

Louis told me the ballet was finished and fine.

I shook my head, agonized, unable to speak.

The stage manager called, "Places, please."

Oh God. Those words. Worse tonight. *Can't do it. Can't.* I felt a thread of sweat slide down my spine. I could not move, I could not breathe. The company lined up in the wings, taking up assigned positions. Louis watched me but I could not meet his eyes.

"Five minutes." The stage manager, again.

Doubt poisoned the air like nerve gas. The stage seemed to spread out like a lake. I swayed and melted to the floor. My gown, the color of rich cream, pooled around me. Couching there, I tried not to weep.

"I. Can't. Go. On." I whispered, "Its. Not. Right."

"You can." Louis grabbed my shoulders. "*You will.*"

Swaying, trying to stand, I felt everyone staring at me.

"For Chrissake," Louis shouted. "On your feet, in position."

"I can't. I won't make fools of these girls in public."

"What the hell do you think you're doing here?"

"Three minutes." The stage manager seemed terrified.

"Do it, Martha." Swiftly, Louis slapped my face. "Now."

I felt the sting — and I felt the bad spell break.

I took my place behind the other dancers.

"Curtain going up," the stage manager called.

I stepped forward. Entered on cue. And danced. Strength flooded into me again, one phrase flowed into another, I felt heat radiate from me, and I was turning, I was bending, I was moving with the others in perfect tempo, as if silk ribbons connect us. Like summer sun, the music seemed to fall across the stage. A moment of tension now. The toughest choreography was just ahead.

Without one missed beat, I went into a spiral fall, bending so far back, one shoulder skimmed the ground. And just as easily, it seemed, I spiraled upward, jack knifing erect again. The curtain came down. The audience response sounded like thunder. Humbled and exhausted now, I held hands with my company and bowed.

As I moved offstage into the wings, I saw the glow of a cigar. As usual, Louis stood beneath a sign that read: *ABSOLUTELY NO SMOKING.* His forehead was beaded with perspiration; a gray cloud hung above his head. The only extra sign of strain was the presence of a second cigar: One in his hand, one clamped in his teeth.

"Good show," he said to each dancer.

"Thank God, thank God," everyone murmured.

"Didn't I tell you so?" Louis hissed at me.

The audience was still on its feet, continuing to applaud, stamping feet, shouting of *Brava, Brava.* The piece had a piercing effect: People stood as one, some cheering in the aisles; the dancers were weeping in the wings. I retreated to my dressing room. I sat in silence, stunned by the power of my own creation. Suddenly I remembered the date: February 2nd. A holy day honoring the Virgin Mary.

The reviews came in. *The New Republic* lauded *Mysteries* for conveying a deep sense of awe and wonder. John Martin, in *The Times,* gave a rave: "Here was a composition which must be ranked among the choreographic masterpieces of the modern dance movement." And for me, John Martin added that I had "already touched the borderland of that mystic territory where greatness dwells." Louis was excited; I remained stunned. At last, drained but dry-eyed, I leaned back against him.

~~~

The next day, Louis took me off to Central Park.

It was a clear blue/white/golden afternoon. Children laughed as they ran toward the park's entrance at 67th Street and Fifth Avenue. I had been coming here alone for years; Louis always wondered why I slipped away each week — and where. A bit jealous, he had finally confronted me.

My response was to take him to the lion cage at the Central Park Zoo. There I told him all about the trips I'd made with my father, long before to the zoo in Pittsburgh. I often called those visits to mind.

Now, in the New York zoo with Louis, my eyes went past the lion's cage to the animal pacing back and forth inside.

"I've always wanted to move like that," I said.

"You do." Louis watched the lion turn. "A marvel."

"Yes. But my first lion had a Death-like gaze."

"Your father taught you not to fear them?"

"Never." Abruptly, my eyes filled. "I was seeing my first dancers."

"And...your father calmed you? When you were frightened?"

"He'd get me to move. I told you how I was after my brother died."

We sat silent for a while, watching the lion's graceful turns.

"Angry at me?" Louis said then. "I didn't know what else to do."

"I was terrible." I shook my head. "Why do you stay with me?"

"Nothing to it. But you can't demoralize the girls. They adore you."

"I'll find a way to make it up to them. You, too, my Luigi. Look."

From my bag, I drew out an apple Danish wrapped in paper.

"The last thing I expected." Louis said. "You still surprise me."

"Too much, maybe. You think we can have some peace now?"

"How boring that would be." Louise smiled. "I give it...six hours."

~~~

Seven, as it turned out. Not far off the mark.

"Oh God," I shrieked just before suppertime.

"Damn," Louis sighed. "Afternoon papers came?"

"Read this review." I shoved the newspaper at him.

"*That* man." Louis frowned. "I never liked him."

"Even so, 'that man' is a respected critic."

"You won over *The Times*. You want them all?"

"I do." I retreated to the bed. "So do you."

"Okay. What does the next smart-ass critic say?"

"When I dance 'I look as if I'm giving birth to a *cube*.' "

"How droll. Why do men try to be such 'wits?' "

"A cube, Louis. A *cube*. No one's said *that* before."

"I'll send him a cube. Ah, you don't think that's funny."

I sank lower in the bed. "There's another one."

Louis grabbed the papers. "Don't read them."

"I have." I went under the covers. "My skin's thin."

"That's not news. Forget it, Martha. Everyone else will."

My eyes showed above the bedclothes. "Can't forget. A cube. Me—"

"We were going out. We were going to a restaurant with *tablecloths*."

I disappeared under the covers. "Not tonight."

"What about me? I need some *gemütlich*. And a drink. Do you ever think of anyone else?"

"I have 'the glooms.' Black and bad. Another night."

"No. Absolutely not. Stop this nonsense. Get up. You're self-indulgent. Come out of that quilt."

My eyes reappeared. "Only under one condition."

"Name it." He pulled the covers off me. "I'll deliver."

"Play me Scott Joplin's 'Maple Leaf Rag'."

Without a word, Louis went to the piano in the empty studio.

If you stood on Tenth Street that evening, you would have heard music coming through an open window; ragtime, sparkling on the air. The music rose into the night, the city and the future.

■

CHAPTER SIX

Abruptly, all the music seemed to stop.

I remembered exactly where I was on October 28th, 1929, when the stock market began to crash. At my studio, I was in rehearsal for a reprise performance of a dance I had created the year before. Louis had composed the score. Ironically, the title of this ballet was *Fragments*.

Clubs closed down. Banks began to fail. Apple-sellers squatted on street corners. Haggard men, staring into space, waited hours for bread. Soup lines stretched for city blocks. I watched boys washing windows for a nickel and women selling apples, two for a nickel.

I hated to dine out, even at the Automat. Whenever I looked up, I saw those faces: small, thin children's faces pressed against the windows. Twice I left in tears, leaving Louis at a table. Beggars pleaded with me for subway fare, a cup of coffee, a crust of bread. The song of the day ran through my head: *Brother, Can You Spare A Dime?*

1932 was like one of my ballets, I thought. Stark. Angular. A series of contrasts. While the country sank deeper into *The Great Depression*, I was awarded a Guggenheim Fellowship for artistic excellence. One of the earliest grants for the arts, this fellowship carried prestige and a decent purse.

As it happened, I was the first American dancer ever to be honored with a Guggenheim, even though the prize was shared with one other artist. Shocked and humbled, I felt very still inside at first, silently wishing my father could be there to see me accept this coveted prize. Then, all at once, my reflective mood passed and I let out a whoop of joy.

Tonight, I told Louis, I would pick up the tab at his favorite restaurant: one with cloth napkins, a rose at every table and a great deal of gemütlich. To my surprise, Louis offered rather gruff congratulations — and the hope that I would use my prize money with some discretion. Hard times were ahead, he reminded me. Louis, always a bit cynical, believed America had more to "fear than fear itself." In 1932, I had vehemently disagreed with him. Then, in 1935, a disturbing incident made me think again.

~~~

"Nazis. *Here.* For *you.* In the studio."

A breathless dancer broke the news to me.

"Not funny." I looked up from my office desk.

"No joke." The dancer gasped. "They're real."

A delegation from Germany's Third Reich had come to call on me one rainy April afternoon. Startled, I quickly changed from my rehearsal clothes to a white jacket and long white skirt. There must be some mistake, I thought. What could this ominous new government want with me and my dancers?

I was more than baffled; I was wary. I received the three-man delegation in the studio's office, where the visitors looked me over. I had more chairs brought in, but before I could offer any sort of refreshment, the Germans wanted to announce their pressing business. One unsmiling young man, intense and thin, did the talking while the others studied me.

The spokesman pushed his tawny hair out of his eyes — eyes with the dull gleam of vintage silver. The emissary's English was somewhat clipped but flawless. Cordial, formal, chilly, he did not linger over pleasantries. With a determined tilt to his chin, he disclosed the nature of his mission to me, "Madame Graham."

As representatives of Adolph Hitler's "glorious regime," the leader said, he and his colleagues had traveled to the United States for a cultural purpose. They had made inquiries about my work and had researched my reputation in the United States. I seemed to be an exponent of American frontier spirit, as well as the new Modernist movement in worldwide art.

The Graham company's press reviews had been carefully examined. Now, this delegation was acting under orders to approach me — and request the honor of my presence at the 1936 Olympic Games to be held in Berlin. I was not the only subject of this great honor; this command performance. My entire company and staff were also requested to be present for this international event. The hosts would choose my repertoire, of course, and review it prior to performance.

Stunned, I watched the faces of my visitors with disbelief and some alarm. The office lights suddenly appeared to be too bright. The air inside the room now felt too close. I called to mind what I already knew about the stirring effect of Hitler's government on Germany and its ethnic pride. There were rumors circulating in America, disturbing rumors, about this leader's rise to power in a new totalitarian state.

Some of us had already heard of the Reich's plans to "eliminate" all people who were not of the "Aryan race." I knew this was not an actual race at all, but rather a fabrication; a demonic and dangerous delusion. The Reich was beginning to round up those it deemed to be "Non-Aryan." Just for "questioning," inquirers were told.

Even so, my Jewish friends had expressed grave concern about the safety of relatives abroad. Some sources reported the quiet disappearance of those questioned. Where? No one knew — not then. But clearly, something ominous and secretive was gaining momentum under orders from the Fuhrer, Adolph Hitler.

His ideology ran counter to everything I believed. At my insistence, Graham was the first racially and ethnically integrated modern dance company in America. I was proud to say I judged artists by our talent. On that basis alone did I take dancers into my company. Though mostly mainstream and white, my troupe included Blacks, Asians, homosexuals, Catholics — and Jews.

Was this not known to the Third Reich? Slowly and precisely, I ticked off these categories for my visitors. Then I repeated the list to be certain it was clear to them. There was some murmuring among the three men; they talked among themselves in German. Then the delegation's leader motioned the others to be silent.

I eyed him; he raked me with his gaze.

The Germans repeated their request.

"Why," I demanded, "would you approach me?"

"You will bring your troupe to the Olympics," I was told.

The words seemed to leave no room for choice. These men did not sound like polite emissaries making diplomatic overtures. They sounded like military officers issuing a direct order. I felt no fear or alarm now; I was infuriated at such arrogance and presumption.

Even if the delegation had been flattering, I would not have wavered for a moment. How could I represent America in Hitler's Berlin?

Now the uneasy pause lengthened in my office. I would have to be frank. I would have to be blunt and clear and unambiguous. If I disappointed my country or the Third Reich, so be it. I looked at each member of the delegation and stated my response in the plainest terms I knew:

"No. I will not dance for Adolf Hitler."

The Germans' leader spoke out., "Your country, Madame Graham. You must represent it."

"I will not. Some of my dancers are Jewish."

There was another murmured consultation among the three representatives. This factor must have escaped their attention and their research. The roster of Graham performers unfolded in my mind but I kept all names to myself. Finally the leader spoke again with a new sense of confidence and resolution.

"They will be totally protected."

My voice was cold. "I decline."

The delegation seemed to wait.

"Perhaps Madame would reconsider?"

"Madame will not." I kept my tone even.

Another pause, so frigid the room turned cold.

"This will be a bad thing for you." The leader snapped at me.

"This will be a bad thing for *you*," I snapped back.

Unescorted, the Third Reich's delegation left the office in a cold and quiet fury.

My studio was silent. I was there alone now. Everyone else had gone home. Retreating to my dressing room, I went over this disturbing confrontation, word for word, reviewing my hasty response. At forty-one, I was no longer a young dancer. I still struggled for funds, despite my nationwide reputation and professional status. And I was almost unknown abroad.

The Germans had been correct in one of their statements: My decision could indeed be bad for me and my company. There would be many missed chances for fame and future opportunities abroad. The Third Reich would certainly have taken care of wide publicity, as would my own country, of course, to showcase American culture.

If I went to the Olympics for America, I would put myself and my entire company on the planet's map, with one deft stroke. All over the world, theatres would open to me and my company. There would be international recognition, invitations for European tours, not to mention monetary rewards. Now, instead, there might be a diplomatic "incident."

My government might resent Graham's refusal to represent America at the Olympics. I went over all these factors in my mind — the benefits refused; the cost of my own quick decision. But could I face myself or my dancers if my troupe performed for Hitler? I knew the answer even as I asked myself that question.

Going would be the mistake.

There's no other way for me.

End of conversation.

~~~

Meanwhile, I had made notes for a new ballet. I thought it would stretch me, my company, my repertoire — and, I hoped, inspire my country as it struggled through the *Great Depression.* I wondered what had given my ancestors the drive to press into a new land, face its dangers, and survive devastating losses? What drove my mother's people to cross an ocean and live through that first lethal winter at the Puritan village of Plymouth? What drove father's people west into the Allegheny Valley mountains?

I recognized the first stage of my creative process: Brooding. It could go on for days or months and I had learned to welcome this phase now. This kind of brooding was nothing like "the glooms" that sank my spirit at times. This was a process akin to a bird settling over new eggs in a nest. Now I began to think beyond my own ancestors.

My mind went beyond them to the settlers who journeyed West in covered wagons, enduring hardship for a promise; only that. Was there still such promise waiting beyond the *Great Depression?* Did these troubled times demand a new migration into an internal landscape where despair could lift? I knew something about that kind of struggle.

As I went through my brooding process, I found myself exploring my own sense of the American spirit: pushing limits, opening new territories, hanging on through hopelessness. And as I began to think how to say all this through movement, I knew I was entering my next creative phase: Experimenting. This area was more difficult than the previous one — those tentative movements expressing my "inner landscape" without words, only with the motion of my own body.

Trying out new steps, new sequences, I found my range expanding. There was something large and expansive about the American experience; this had to be a dance that overcame vast distances. For the first time, I realized I needed a scenic designer to give the piece a reference point, a horizon line. And I knew precisely whom I wanted. Not a traditional set designer. Someone who could carve out space: the renowned Japanese-American sculptor, Isamu Noguchi.

I hoped we would understand each other and we did. Immediately. With *Frontier,* the new ballet, we began a collaboration lasting decades. Noguchi's affinity for spare Asian forms, negative space, and the ritual of Kabuki Theatre made a natural fit with my own artistic vision. I admired Noguchi's spare aesthetic sense; his way of peeling shapes down to our essentials, as I did with dance.

Noguchi was also pleased to know how well I understood his timeless images, his value of "the void" as well as "the object." This artistic collaboration was so successful, Noguchi reserved his theatrical work only for me, and later, Merce Cunningham. The great sculptor would work with no other dancers, even as his reputation grew. Merce and I never took this honor for granted.

For my new ballet, Noguchi had designed a rail fence, two poles and strung between them, two long ropes in a V-formation. I, the soloist, was not really dancing alone, I knew. I was in physical dialogue with Noguchi's set and Louis Horst's score, spare, abstract, and percussive; its snare drum seemed a call to arms, a summons to courage.

In a costume of my own design, I was a pioneer woman. I stretched one foot to the top rail of Noguchi's fence, and stretched my other foot to touch the ground. Gazing out into the illusion of great distance, I abandoned the sober expression that had marked my previous performances. The change in my face made a stunning impression.

In *Frontier*, I smiled with confidence and optimism — a smile so radiant, it drew praise from Walter Terry, a prominent critic, who called my expression "ravishing." That, he wrote, reflected the hope of a pioneer looking out over new terrain, as I had wanted to convey it. Terry also felt that this ballet would affect the shape of theatre in the future.

As I stretched against Noguchi's abstract version of a rail fence, I reached for earth and sky at once, making myself a bridge to the future. I lived into the role of pioneer, projecting joy through a series of leaps, and confidence through a seamless series of steps forward. This new dance looked beyond devastation to a new horizon line. With Noguchi's set and Louis's spare, stirring score, *Frontier* viewers were reminded of America's promise. Or so I hoped.

Frontier premiered at the Guild Theatre on April 28th, 1935, to a grand reception by patrons and press. I felt the rightness of this dance as I moved through it. Each movement conveyed the strength of our pioneering spirit — and better times beyond the current darkness. The reviews, thank God, were raves.

~~~

A new invitation arrived two years later.

This time it came from 1600 Pennsylvania Avenue. Stunned again, I stared at the embossed envelope in my hand. President and Mrs. Roosevelt had requested the honor of my presence and performance — at the White House in Washington, D.C. Miss Graham would be the first American dancer to receive this honor, which included an "informal dinner" with the Roosevelt themselves.

I swallowed hard. This command performance paid tribute to my achievements, I knew, but it also meant far more than that. This was a tribute to the art of dance itself and to all American dancers. Again, it might cause resentment from my peers — but it would also open the way for them to similar honors. Meanwhile, I must perform solo, without my company around me; only Louis was invited to accompany me on the piano.

If I did well enough, dance itself might cease to be a stepchild of the arts. So much depended on the impression I might make on the First Family — I felt dizzy, thrilled, and disbelieving all at once. If "Miss Ruth" could see me now — no longer too short, too old, too ugly for a command performance in the East Room. But terror soon replaced my sense of vindication.

When our train pulled into Union Station in Washington, D.C., I was so scared and stunned, I felt as if I moved underwater, slowed, silent, in a strange new element. Our host had sent a car and driver for us; thoughtful, formal service.

As we passed the bone-white Capitol dome, I tried not to gape like a child. My hands felt cold inside my gloves and my pulse ticked fast. Ahead lay the visit, the dinner — the performance. These twenty-four hours could win recognition for the world of dance. Or not. For the Graham company. Or not. For a doctor's daughter from Pennsylvania. Or not. I felt distinctly nauseated.

From the sedan's window, I watched the city blur around me. I seemed to observe another Martha and another Louis passing through the White House gates. And then, somehow, we were swept inside the building by the Head Usher who welcomed us and motioned for a butler. I can only recall what seemed like miles of red carpeting and a slight echo. Maybe it was the buzzing in my ears.

Our bags had vanished into the depths of the great house. All but one of the American presidents had lived here, I told myself. Lincoln had lain in state here, in the room where I would dance. *And I am here.* Anyone who was not awed by such a visit would be dead or lying, Louis whispered to me. We had not walked into a picture postcard of the White House. *This is it*, I whispered back. *This is happening.*

The invitation was for dinner with the First Family and friends upstairs in "The Residence." My throat had closed from nervous tension. The very thought of swallowing seemed impossible to me. Dinner would be followed by the dance program itself, downstairs in the East Room.

I was escorted to my White House chamber where I sat in an upholstered chair, gazing out at the Rose Garden. I did my warmup stretches but was too nervous to join the Presidential party for dinner. I missed my only chance to dine with the Roosevelts. Louis certainly did not.

He made my excuses: Miss Graham was in the midst of preparation for tonight's performance. Actually, he guessed, Miss Graham was in the midst of throwing up. To calm his own nerves, Louis admitted to me, he had taken a long swig of Bourbon from the bottle he had wrapped in a plain paper bag and hidden in his suitcase. How embarrassing to find a White House butler had laid out his things and no doubt, had discovered the hidden bottle — which, if course, was never mentioned.

After scanning the performance space and the piano, Louis checked back with me. On the flowered carpet, I sat cross-legged, spine straight, trying to breathe deeply. *Contract...Release....* Louis left me undisturbed and looked for the shower in the room he thought was his. When Louis opened the shower door, he almost walked in on the President's son, Elliot, wet and naked as a seal. Louis crept back to the right room for another swig of Bourbon before dinner.

In costume, I opened my door to the Head Usher's knock. He did not blink at my outfit; he simply escorted my down a staircase, through a hallway, then another, and then the East Room's doors were opened before me. Mrs. Roosevelt greeted me with such informality and warmth, I almost lost my nervousness. But then she led me to the President, waiting in his chair and flanked by friends. We greeted one another, though I could never recall the exact words we spoke.

Nor did I notice the braces on the President's legs; I only saw that face, that tilted chin, that glint of spectacles. This was the man who stared out at me from the newspapers almost every day; a face almost as familiar as my father's. And the President's welcoming voice, also oddly familial; I had heard it every week or more on my Zenith radio.

For a moment, the great room swam before my eyes. Then the professional within me took over. There was no stage, so I moved to the center of the parquet floor where I would dance barefoot. A White House Usher introduced "Miss Martha Graham ac-companied by Mr. Louis Horst." Unflappable, some-how, Louis took his place behind me, to the right, at the concert grand piano.

For my opening piece I had selected *Frontier*. Now my "signature solo," its pioneering American theme seemed right for the White House presentation. But as I stepped forward, I felt myself freeze inside. Once Osamu Noguchi had soothed my stage fright by speaking to me in his quiet voice, "Just dance it for me, all right? Dance as if there's no one here but us."

Dance as if there's no one here but us. I leaned back against Isamu's rail fence.. *Just for me, Martha.* But I was gone. The movements grew stronger, spiraling from feet to head, and I was no longer Martha; the pioneer woman of *Frontier* had replaced me. At the end, I gave my smile of promise, hope, and optimism to the President of the United States.

After two more pieces and a strong round of applause, it was time for a graceful departure. Mrs. Roosevelt rose to offer me another warm embrace. She was a tall woman, broad through the shoulders. I was tiny as a child in her strong arms. I looked into the First Lady's eyes, pressed her hands, and we were escorted out to our waiting car.

Even now, our time at the White House has the quality of a daydream, a young dancer's fantasy — not entirely real. As we rode north on the train, I wondered how I could share my White House debut with my fellow dancers. All I could do, Louis said, was to open the way for them.

"You did good," he said then.

"*We* did, Louis." I breathed evenly again.

~~~

With Roosevelt's new administration, I sensed a shift in the atmosphere, the way I did on September days when the air turned crisp. Government agencies were taking steps to create employment. I found myself watching the news when the Works Progress Administration went into action. The WPA, as everyone called it, offered jobs and subsidies for artists, from architects to actors.

But why not dancers? I aimed my question at the invisible broadcaster whose voice came through my Zenith radio. Dancers were yet to be included — not for long, I hoped. Why must we be classed with strippers in bawdy houses on 42nd Street? Always concerned for my company, I struggled to keep up its funding throughout those lean years. I made little money from my teaching but it yielded rewards in other ways.

I was not yet adroit about publicity. When I gave movement classes at *The Neighborhood Playhouse*, I would not let myself be photographed with them for my own purposes — even with such stars as Mickey Rooney, Eli Wallach, Anne Jackson, and Marlon Brando. I saw my role clearly: as an artist, a dancer, and a movement coach for dramatic artists. They worked so hard to show emotion through gesture as well as words. I felt awkward about exploiting them as contacts.

I felt the same way about Helen Keller, a celebrity by then. When she chose to visit the Graham studio, I was moved, honored — and baffled. Deaf and blind from infancy, Miss Keller had learned to do far more than speak and write; she was now a lecturer, an author, and she spoke out for people with impairments.

But what could a dancer offer to someone who lived in a dark and silent world? When Miss Keller arrived at the Graham studio, she resolved this dilemma for me in an instant. She simply took off her shoes during a dance and felt its vibrations coming from the floor and through her feet.

Next, she asked me to explain the act of jumping; a confusing concept. I positioned Helen's hands on the torso of a dancer who held still, then began to jump. Helen's hands moved up and down with the leaping body; I saw joy break over her face like a sudden splash of sunlight. Raising her arms into the air on her own, Helen Keller fairly crowed. I could not use this connection for gain; knowing Helen Keller seemed gain enough.

"Times are tough," Louis reminded me again. That they were, I said. With reluctance, I thought through a list of friends I might approach for funding. Finally a name came to me. Here was one person who could afford a contribution to the arts. A longtime Graham admirer, Katherine Cornell was not only a great actress, she sympathized with performers' needs. In addition, Miss Cornell had inherited a fortune from her father, a physician who just happened to invent the windshield wiper. The First Lady of the Stage became a generous Graham benefactor.

~~~

Can I do this? I wondered, took a breath, and called the impresario, S.L. Rothafel, as he was opening his newest theatre: Radio City Music Hall. I wangled a spot on the playbill for my troupe. The theatre was overly ornate, to my mind, and the Rockettes' kick-line dominated the program.

The Graham company was stuck as Number 18 on the program, near the end of the long gala. The dance went well, I thought, but it did not suit the music hall's audience. I was neither stricken or surprised when my deal with Rothafel broke down. I continued to make do with teaching, where I felt rewarded in other ways.

One of the most gifted of "The Graham girls," noted how quiet I had seemed at first — a small woman who appeared to hide inside a deep cloche hat; I cut a stylish figure, but I said little and seemed shy. That impression changed as soon as I stepped before the class and began to speak.

I was unaware of the effect I had; even so, my presence seemed to be so strong, students swore they could sense it without turning around to look at the teacher entering from the back of the studio. One ofmy principle dancers, John Butler put it simply "You would kill for Martha," he said.

~~~

As the Nazis' power grew, more disturbing reports reached me in New York and even in New England, where I summered during much of the Thirties. Amid Vermont's green hills lay a newly founded college for women: Bennington, it was called, offering a liberal arts program with a decided emphasis on the creativity, self-expression, and the arts.

It was there that one of my former students started the first Department of Dance in an American academic setting — and Bennington welcomed me every summer through much of the Thirties; I could have free room and board, a small stipend, and the freedom to teach dance to selected students. Louis taught music and together we motored north to take up residence at the college, housed in the main building of a grand old estate once owned by the wealthy Jennings family.

There, amid Vermont's rolling hills, I quickly settled in. The morning air was moist and fresh. Cows lowed and loitered under great shade trees. The gentle slope of Mount Anthony lifted my eyes and when I lowered them I saw meadows glimmering with wild flowers. Usually an urban person, I settled easily into the rural peace of this place, far from the steaming pavements of New York in July and August.

Bennington began to draw on a broad range of talent from the dance world: Charles Weideman, Doris Humphrey, Hanya Holm, Jose Limon. Though we clashed at times, this gathering formed a rare artistic community. Soon it was further enriched by the modern composer, John Cage, teaching music theory, John Martin, teaching dramatic criticism and scholar Joseph Campbell lecturing on Greek mythology.

As the world seemed to slide closer to darkness, I felt an urgent need for a retreat to Bennington. Perhaps this summer's setting might ease the strain on my relationship with Louis. When had it started? Sometime after our trip to New Mexico, I thought, on my grant money from the Guggenheim Foundation.

Could Louis, with so much of his own talent, resent my award? Was he envious of my growing success? The White House invitation? Or had I exhausted Louis's patience with my anguish over *Primitive Mysteries?* Perhaps the trouble was a combination of many pent-up feelings.

If only I could understand Louis's thinking, I felt I could mend whatever was breaking down between us. One evening, as we sat silent in my crowded bedroom,

I touched his face and he turned away. No big gesture. Just enough to prompt me to speak.

"What is it, my Luigi?" My voice was soft.

"What is '*it*,' Martha?" He seemed to mock me.

"What's wrong between us? You're angry at me?"

"Maybe *you're* angry at *me*, no?" He deftly parried.

"Let's not fence, Louis. I want you to tell me."

"Not now." He turned away. "I have work to do."

The distance began to widen between us: first a crack too small to notice, then the kind of gap you would find in an uneven stretch of paving. You'd simply step over it, of course, but then the gap grew wider — too large to breach. Now Louis seemed to be a figure in the middle distance, still present but not near enough to touch. I saw myself calling out to him but the words were lost somewhere in the air between us.

Our intimacy at work, at meals, in bed seemed to evaporate, like a slow leak in a tire. But why? And how? The changes were so slow to come, so subtle, I had not noticed our pattern, our progression until the last few months. If I'd noticed sooner, I would have said we were only going through a rough patch, a phase, like any married couple. Except we were not married. I could never quite forget that.

"Is something bothering you?" a friend once asked me while Louis was in the room. Until that moment we had been enjoying a visit over tea and scones, butter and fresh raspberry preserves. I could put on a good face when I had to but I had not fooled this friend, nor had I fooled another, just a week before.

Now my friend persisted. "Tell me."

"Frustrated in bed," Louis broke in.

Of course, this was taken as a joke — a crude one; a mean one, I thought. It also put a stop to further questions from well-meaning friends. Whenever a question touched on my well-being, Louis answered for me with that same phrase. It worked every time. But not on me.

I would often excuse myself and take a taxi to St. Patrick's Cathedral, where I felt calmer, safe from wounding words, cradled in the nave's pooling blue light. I went there often; never to attend Mass, of course, only to light candles and to weep in privacy.

There I was not likely to run into anyone I knew. There I felt safe and soothed by the great cathedral's holy hush. There, I thought of Lizzie Prendergast: my strength, my comfort; her way of getting everyone through loss or pain. In St. Patrick's "Lady Chapel," I conjured up Lizzie's image and those early, furtive excursions to my forbidden church.

At Bennington, however, I never felt the need to flee to sacred space. It was already there. At dawn and dusk, that holy hush was all around me and it seemed to cause a change in Louis, as well. They were both at peace in Vermont, as if we'd crossed some line into a mystical realm like Camelot.

I was sensitive to the power of place. Vermont was one of those locales that generated peace. All I had to do was inhale the smell of its lush grass and my spirit was eased. There we never quarreled about anything, as if Bennington exercised some pastoral magic over us.

In that setting, I could try to forget the whispered rumors from well-meaning friends — rumors of my partner's infidelities, however brief, with my own students. The girls he chose were always nineteen, it seemed, sweet, tentative, and great admirers of Louis. They thought of him as far more than our musical director; he was a mentor, a protector, a man about town, a man of the world — as he once was to me.

I had even noticed some flirtations recently in class — before my eyes, at my own studio. I'd tried to tell myself it wasn't really flirting, it wasn't really serious; only banter, only tension breaking, only laughter lingering a bit too long. If there was anything more to it, this was serious business. But, it could not be serious. Could it?

Whenever Louis and I had a quarrel, I could count on a flirtation starting up at the piano during the very first session of the very next morning. And who was I to put claims on Louis? After all, I was not his wife. It began to look as if I would never be that. All discussions of divorce still ended in explosions. The flirtations did not put such demands on him.

The girls were innocents, I knew, just as virginal and vulnerable as I had been at Denishawn when Louis had first wooed and won me. Perhaps he gravitated to young and vulnerable dancers; I had never noticed this before. Perhaps I'd avoided such observations until now.

But surely I was only imagining any after-hours depth to such exchanges. Louis was far too busy for such wanderings. He was working often now at night as a musical conductor for some orchestra he never named. So he said. I chose not to investigate the matter. I also tried not to read too much into Louis's apparent attraction to a young dancer, thirty years his junior, and a member of the Graham company.

Alone and awake at three in the morning, I would sit up at my typewriter, working out new ideas or copying lines of poetry that spoke to me. The brighter ones, the braver verses, seemed more difficult for me to find lately. I had to avoid Poe, of course, and the lines of love penned by Elizabeth Barrett Browning. The list grew longer every week.

One night, I turned to a poem that had always lifted black moods for me: Emily Dickinson's, "Hope is the Thing with feathers."

Although I was a stalwart admirer of Emily Dickinson, I tore that page out of my poetry book, crumpled the paper and tossed it in the trash. I knew I'd not be seeing Louis until we met at the studio the next day.

One night, alone again, I typed myself a note:

YOU'VE LIED TO YOURSELF FOR YEARS.

Then I burned the page in the kitchen sink.

Perhaps Louis was only panicked by his entrance into his fifties and, if so, I believed that crisis would pass. Other men went through that time of life in the same way: the self-absorption, the dalliances with other women, the need to see adoration on fresh young faces. It was easy to explain — but hard to take it calmly.

~~~

Meanwhile, my spirit craved a peaceful space where I could create dance again. In Vermont, I had always felt serene yet stimulated by the artistic ferment all around my. At Bennington, I always seemed to be poised at the edge of magical idea, open space for creation, another intriguing new frontier.

I could dream a pioneer woman into movement, art, and dance. I could design and sew my own distinctive costumes. I could inspire countless students. I could invent hours of choreography. I could even make a decent pot roast if I chose. But I could not choreograph the wisest steps for my life.

Now, as I look back over its decades, I'm dismayed to see the same mistakes repeat themselves, the same destructive patterns reappearing. I was opening new frontiers each year in my art, but was my own story only one of spirals? I did not know. I chose to see it as an upward graph, another frontier — it seemed less painful that way.

I could not know how dangerous the next "frontier" would be for me. There seemed some reason to see good times ahead; I sensed no swerves or detours ahead — only a sense of promise and the opening of new terrain.

When I entered it, I knew, there would be a shine to that new inviting territory: a sense of promise and renewal, as most frontiers display at first. Our perils seldom reveal themselves immediately and when they do, they come at you from behind.

I knew all this. I knew myself better than anyone could guess. And I knew my craft too well to ignore one basic fact: The risk of a dangerous and daring leap can seem so easy to avoid — until a sinew snaps.

■

CHAPTER SEVEN

I did not see it coming.

Everyone else did, I suspect.

Only now, looking back, do I recognize the chore-ographer's "floor pattern" I had set down for my future. If I'd written out one of my usual synopses for the stage, I might have made the crucial changes just in time. An expert at scenarios, I could sense a story's arc. How it would start. How it would crest. Before I knew its steps, I always knew how a work would end.

But not this time.

I was too close to the storyline.

I was plotting life, not art. My own.

This new scenario was cast for trouble.

Enter: The heroine, a middle-aged diva.

Exit: Her mentor with a younger woman.

Enter: A younger handsome man.

Notes: With this new man, it seemed, lay the heroine's last chance for love and marriage. What would she do with it? Would she let it pass and press on alone, wedded only to the dance? Would she sense ulterior motives in the younger man? Or would she house him at the epicenter of her world?

Looking back, the heroine's choice seems predictable, the ending of the piece inevitable. But foresight, in this case, tends to be unclear. It is always something of a trickster, manipulating hopes and fears. Didn't it always work like that? The heroine asks herself much later. Too late, she might have added. Much too late.

~~~

Why? Friends asked.

Why Erick Hawkins?

Why not? I'd retort.

He had the body of a Greek god. He was an accomplished dancer. Muscular, and single, Erick was the opposite of portly, paternal, married Louis Horst, who happened to be otherwise engaged at the time. When Erick's troupe danced at Bennington, my attraction to him was immediate. According to his program notes, he was trained at Harvard in the classics and by Balanchine in ballet. Erick was only twenty-nine that summer, fifteen years my junior — a fact he did not know.

We met on a starry August night in 1938; I made sure I went backstage to praise his performance. Flushed and flattered, he, in turn, had praise for my own work. He had seen me in *Frontier*; that had caused his shift from ballet to modern dance. We wished each other well. I remember we shook hands. As I left his dressing room, I wondered if I would see this man again.

Erick Hawkins made quite certain that I did.

Early in September he appeared at my studio. Attentively, he took in everything: the floor, the barre, the dancers, the lack of mirrors on the walls. We spoke of mutual friends and mutual acquaintances. Erick was finished with the New York City Ballet. It was time for him to move on and make his mark somewhere else. He wondered if he might sit in on my classes, simply to observe my artistic sense, I saw no harm in that.

I should have. Looking back now this is clear. It was the time-worn temptation: Middle-aged diva on the rebound, flattered by a younger man's attention. Young man on the ladder, flattered by the diva's attraction. She wants love, he wants fame. An even trade; so it seems to him. Of course I didn't see any calculations then. I didn't recognize Erick's driving ambition; he was so eager to do humble chores. Slowly, gradually, he made himself useful around the studio.

He became the first male dancer to take classes there. The girls resented this. He did not seem to mind. From a distance, he appeared aloof, even arrogant. Up close, he seemed dedicated and frankly, delicious. When he asked me to coach him in the Graham Technique, I did not hesitate. I saw no harm in that. I should have. Again. By this time, however, I was beyond reason, logic, warnings, common sense.

Predictably enough, our after-hour coaching sessions ended in short walks, long talks, coffee cooling in our cups.

"You're worried about the girls," he said.

"They'll get over it. Suppose I add another man."

"Good. That would take the heat off me."

"You dance like a veteran of Graham."

"Aw shucks." He smiled. "Good coach."

"My first dance was in church," I said.

"Mine was in an empty Colorado barn."

"What did you like to read the most?"

"Greek myths." He laughed. "Like you."

We shared our love of the classics. We shared our love of autumn, our hatred of summer, a craving for raw honey, a belief in luck.

"And the girls say we have nothing in common." We had to laugh at that. We laughed together openly at Bennington, that next summer. Many colleagues seemed oblivious. Some, like Louis, noticed.

"Be careful," he cautioned me.

"Of what, exactly?" I demanded.

"Young usurpers," he snapped back.

"You're a fine one to talk, aren't you?"

"I see an older woman with a gigolo—"

"No gigolo." I slapped Louis's face.

"I had it coming." He lumbered off.

"I guess you did," I shouted after him.

He did not turn or look back at me.

After the summer session ended, I stayed on for a few days of private time with Erick. Around us the maples burst into their annual red blaze. It never rained during that time. The sky was an electric blue. After I told Erick about the blue and red Kadinsky I so loved, we drove into Boston and he bought me a print of the painting. I stared at it, unable to speak. No one had ever given me such a gift.

He was becoming indispensable to me.

~~~

"Indispensible."

If you said that around the Graham studios in 1940, anyone and everyone would have answered: You must mean Erick Hawkins.

Even his detractors grudgingly admitted it: Erick had earned that description, taking over much of the

Graham company's management — and freeing me up for more creative work. This Hawkins fellow seemed almost too good, too willing, too eager to take over business details, people said. I did not see it that way, however.

I was relieved and grateful: my life was less frantic and more liberated than it had been in years. Time for my own dancing expanded; I worked out new choreography while Erick oversaw the necessary workings of a production company: building sets, storing costumes, taking inventories, scheduling classes, rehearsals and performances.

Erick also attended to our constant need for funding. I had approached Katherine Cornell for a few hundred dollars out of her immense fortune. Erick, with a blend of city savvy and "aw shucks" Western charm approached Miss Cornell for thousands — and got them. Easily. Cordially. Without damage to my friendship with Katherine. Graham's bank balance leapt higher.

Next, Erick turned to his old friend, Lincoln Kirstein, heir to yet another fortune; this one from the famed department store, Filene's. Soon another source of funding opened up for the Graham school and dance troupe. Louis had never been so bold or so financially adept. I had carried the burden of business alone.

Even so, the company did not hide its hostility to Erick, seen as a male interloper on a female preserve. Every day, he joined us for class, and every day, he was ignored. I heard the murmurings in the halls.

"What's he doing here?" the dancers whispered.

"He watches her," said tall, lean Faye.

"How she looks at him," said blue-eyed Nan.

"He's a fine dancer though, I've watched."

"He's a cliche! It's the old show-biz game."

"Older woman, younger man, out for himself?"

"Don't be a cynic. He seems very sincere."

"Don't they all, at first." Nan ruffled her red hair.

I didn't care what anyone said. I was in full-bloom then: womanly yet girlish, my body firm, my face still smooth. Long before, Louis said my mouth looked like a rose starting to open. If I may say so, I appeared younger than my years. I moved easily, like a woman in her prime.

Erick was the reason, I knew. He had a flat two blocks away from mine, but it was merely a postal address to him. His clothes were in my drawers. His shaving soap was on my shelf. His robe hung on my bedroom door.

~~~

From time to time, Erick and I stole away together for a few days in New Mexico. Our city world, our studio and its demands — all left behind. We were only for each other there. At night, we often slept outside and made love in the open air, feeling the breezes against our arms and legs, as we wrapped around each other.

I liked to lie in Erick's arms and gaze up at spangled skies, where the stars seemed closer than anywhere else. The air cooled quickly in the evenings but I felt the heat from this lion of a man, whose muscles rippled underneath his skin as he moved rhythmically against me. We touched off something fierce, almost forbidden, in each other — a wildness for which we had no words.

At dusk, I sat cross-legged, leaning back against Erick, heated again by the warmth of his body. Together we watched the rising moon, a slice of silver hanging in skies, the color of ripe plums. Venus glowed just below it: "the evening star," magnetized, it seemed, to the moon as it waxed. To me the sliver was a dagger, masculine and potent, while Venus was a female form, round and brilliant, drawn to the silver knife.

As lovers we felt no need to seek out entertainment: friends, restaurants in Santa Fe, great festivals on its central plaza. We chose to be alone together in a lean-to cabin, sleeping outside or enveloped in a patchwork quilt on an iron bedstead. Every evening, from a rocking chair on the porch, I watched Erick spear a steak and cook it over open flames.

He would stab the meat with swift strokes, just the way he killed a snake one afternoon, as we walked a dirt road. I remembered Erick chopping off its head, its tail, and cutting the body into pieces. I had held my breath as I watched the creature's death-spiral, its reflexive twitching; then its absolute destruction, piece by piece. I turned away, gagging, when I saw translucent scales shimmer in the dust.

"Was it poisonous?" I asked at last.

"It was a snake," he said; that was all.

"But was it all that dangerous?"

"It was a snake," he said again.

"But Erick—" I began and stopped.

"If it's in the way, it goes." His face was set.

"Let's go back. I'll shake up some Margaritas."

"That's the girl I love." He hoisted me into the air.

On these excursions, Erick was in his native element; I tried to keep that in mind. He knew this territory far better than I did. This was his turf, not so far from the Colorado town where he was born. Even so, that night I dreamed about the snake. The gleaming ax. The stunning blows. The thrill and danger coiled within such savagery.

When I awoke at midnight, I was trembling. Beside me, Erick slept on, the curve of one broad shoulder caught in a shaft of moonlight. His skin was silvery; his face was lit. Was he a shining tempter, beautiful as Lucifer? The seducer who sapped the heroine of her gift, her powers? *Foolishness,* I scolded myself. *Don't make this into another myth.* Erick was a man, not a fallen angel. A sensual, insatiable man, pulling me back into his arms even as I thought of him. We ignited each other, got white-hot together, slick and wild.

Every evening Erick stood silhouetted against his red/gold fire, turning steaks and ignoring the strange laughter of coyotes. He did not even pause to look around; the pitch of the coyotes' cries told him how to gauge how near we were. He would never let anything happen to me, I told myself. He was Prometheus Unbound, primal Man, fire-starter, fierce protector, and later, in our creaky bed, fire itself.

After each of these interludes, when Erick and I returned to New York City and the Greenwich Village studio, our bond always seemed stronger. In fact, it was. There were no reports about the Western journeys, but lovers have their secrets. Certain smiles would pass from him to me and back again. Clearly, we shared very private memories. Close together, we made heat. That was all anyone at Graham really knew. There were no travel photos to show, no adventures — at least for the telling. These sojourns were out of bounds and out of anybody's reach. No one understood our coupling, but as a couple we really did not care.

~~~

She's under his spell, the girls whispered.

You don't understand, I wanted to say.

He's under hers: The whispering went on.

You've never felt like this, I thought

He'll ruin her life, the Graham girls predicted.

"Too much gossip lately," I scolded them all.

The girls were stony-faced and unyielding no matter what Erick said. He did not seem to belong here, this "All American Boy" from Colorado, with a bit of Western swagger left in his long stride. He even asked if he might have a walkon part some time. No harm in that, I told myself. A masculine presence added a new dynamic to the studio. "Grow up," I told the girls. "Erick's not competing with you."

In fact, at the beginning, he had struggled with the daily class work. This was a source of unspoken delight throughout the troupe. Despite his ballet training and muscular physique, Erick was not as fit and taut and flexible as "the Graham Girls."

He had to work long and hard to learn my demanding technique — and he did, practicing after hours as I once did at Denishawn. Gradually Erick began to master the rigorous movements and sequences. That was when I began to coach him after hours. In the studio office we were careful to talk business. Except one day.

"You're worried about the girls," he said.

"They'll get over it. I just didn't expect a turf war."

"Add another man, maybe? Take the heat off me?"

"It's good to have a strong ally," I sighed.

"You do." He touched my inner thigh.

"Don't," I said. "Not here."

"Here?" He moved his hand higher and this time I did not protest. I had always fled intense romance; I feared it would dilute my work. But my fear gave way to Erick's passion. It all started with those private coaching sessions. He was eager, responsive, and always, admiring.

~~~

I felt lighter than I could remember. Lighter — and braver. Always one to stretch my borders, I paced through many nights before I made an unsettling decision. I knew best how Erick had progressed in the unique Graham style of dance. If he could be my first male soloist, the troupe would have a more extensive repertoire. But first, I knew, there would be anger, even rage, over this innovative step.

One Monday morning, I gathered everyone together in the studio, dancers, students and staff. There was a tense silence as the late arrivals darted in. I stood before "the Graham girls" and braced myself.

"We need to broaden our range as a company," I began. "Sometimes that's not easy. I'm announcing a hard choice. It will be unpopular, I know, until we all get used to it. And that may take some time."

"Here it comes," a seasoned dancer muttered.

"And there we go," another dancer echoed.

"I'm announcing the addition of a male soloist to our company." I felt something like electricity streak through the studio. "This opens the way for other men as well. I've always been proud to run an integrated company — in every way except for gender. That needs to change."

I paused to take a breath. "I've invited Erick Hawkins to join us. He will be a principle soloist because he'll play all the male roles. I believe in his natural gifts as well." I paused to draw another breath and steady my voice. "If you can't live with my decision, you may leave at any time. You'll be missed. That's all. It's time for class."

Before I'd finished, a dancer had stormed out.

I expected a strong reaction — and I got it.

Four veteran dances so resented this newcomer's leap ahead of them, they quit. On the spot. For good. Many who remained did not try to hide their hostility toward Erick. Within his hearing, they called him "The Torso," mocking his muscular appeal. But Sophie Maslow, already a principle dancer, was one of the few "Graham girls" to approve of Erick — and my choice. He touched it out, strong and silent: Western style, she said.

Wounded as I was by four rejections, I felt I had led my company in the right direction. I had to keep moving Graham forward even if I'd taken a tough stance. In one of my late night prowls, I recalled a statement I'd once made to Louis. I preferred approval to hostility but I preferred hostility to mere indifference. Here, now, was the acid test. Did I mean it? Could I take it? The challenge was now.

I held this stance as I braced myself to take a new step forward. I dared to add another man to my troupe: A "natural" named Merce Cunningham. Also a Westerner, he was a prize discovery at only twenty years of age: wildly talented, witty and inventive. Merce managed to win the admiration of "The Graham Girls," with his creativity and humor — and the highest leaps anyone had ever seen. His charm endured, even when he got the lead in the next new ballet, my first comedic piece, *Every Soul Is A Circus*.

More men joined up with Graham and, as I had expected, the furor over gender faded out. After months of upheaval, my company was completely integrated and stable. As the Thirties ended, the troupe had five men and nine women; blacks, whites, and Asians. Graham was the first American dance company to cross racial lines, and now, dating back to 1926, it was the oldest modern dance toupe in the country.

My own style was growing in response to the male dancers. My choreography was lighter now, more fluid, less vehement. I smiled often in performance; my sense of humor showed and I felt I moved with a new ease.

To everyone's surprise and delight, I added a wide range bright colors to my costumes for the first time. Before this, we had always danced in black and white. Only once, had I danced in purple; only once in red. Now we were green and blue and gold and striped. Of course this change reflected how I felt inside.

These colors were in evidence when the company presented my first "dance-drama," *Letter To The World,* a tribute to the great American poet, Emily Dickinson. The production was based a new theme for me: the deep pull of love. There had been a serious romance in Dickinson's life, conducted over years of correspondence. It was ecstasy; it was agony, of course, as well. This was what caught and held my attention now. *Letter to the World* was an instant classic and a stunning success.

~~~

The flourishing Graham company moved into a larger studio at 66 Fifth Avenue. Nearby but separate, my new apartment was a top-floor aerie in a brownstone, far more private than my other residences. There was a reason for the change in my living arrangements. For the first time, I wanted to keep my personal and professional life separate. I wanted a sanctuary for my life with Erick.

Still ambitious, encouraged by good press, Erick approached my closest friend, the choreographer Agnes de Mille. She was working on a new musical slated for a Broadway premiere.   The score had already been written and arranged by the great Richard Rodgers, with lyrics by Oscar Hammerstein II. The "book" — the script — was finished. Auditions had begun for a ground-breaking musical eagerly.   Its title was *Oklahoma!*

"Can you get me a reading?" Erick asked Agnes.

She was a bit taken aback by his brashness.

"Well, would you put in a word?" He pressed.

My loyal friend managed to wangle an audition for Erick; he wanted to dance in the show but he also wanted to read for a speaking part. Together he and Agnes entered the Broadhurst Theatre, where auditions were in progress. These proceeded under the watchful eye of Richard Rodgers himself, as well as the show's director and producer.

"I'll do the first song," Erick announced.

"You'll read" the stage manager snapped.

"I'll improvise." Erick began to sing.

Richard Rodgers abruptly left the theatre.

"Audition's over." The stage manager snarled.

"Explain that, Erick" Agnes demanded.

He was unfazed. "Just trying to get in the door."

Horrified, Agnes chalked this episode up to Erick's arrogance; she'd always suspected him of that. I could not explain his behavior that simply. I knew he wasn't stupid; arrogance was the only other choice. When I heard about the incident I said nothing but found myself making up mental excuses for Erick's behavior. He was inexperienced, he was nervous, excited, eager, possibly confused, I told myself. But he had traded on my name and my friend's name as well. That thought outweighed all the others.

Losing control, I raged at Erick in the office.

"How could you embarrass Agnes?" I hissed.

"I have to make my own way." He shot back.

"And didn't I? You were rude, out of bounds."

"You're not pretty as a scold," Erick lashed back.

"You're not the only one aiming for the top."

"At least you know my direction," he slammed out.

~~~

Everyone in the studio tried to ignore the row; it passed before the day was over. Erick pressed on to raise more funds and make new contacts: one of these paid off in a way far greater than anyone could have imagined.

A young French woman joined the Graham classes: a shy brunette, lisping slightly, she registered only as "Bethsabee." Erick set about tracking down the girl's identity. The young woman's last name was de Rothschild; she was a member of the world-famous banking family. She had not wanted any "special treatment."

Sweet-spirited and gentle, she was entranced by me, for some reason, as well as the Graham approach to dance. I returned her growing devotion. Bethsabee had escaped from France with her family just before the Nazis took Paris. Now ensconced in New York, she found great comfort in the arts, especially dance.

Our friendship grew; I never would have approached Bethsabee for contributions. Erick would — and did. Soon the company's funds were richly increased and Erick was proud. I had mixed feeling about the gift and told Bethsabee this when I thanked her for her generosity.

"*C'est rien.*" She smiled.

"It is not 'nothing,' darling."

"Friendship is all," she said.

"Yes. Friendship and dance."

"How did you choose your calling?"

"I didn't choose. It chose me."

~~~

Another new ballet was going well. Its brooding tone was well suited to the wartime atmosphere. I was well aware of the country's mood. As a volunteer for the Red Cross, I wrote monthly letters to several American soldiers stationed abroad. For me, the war itself was a subject too sensitive to translate into dance. Instead, I returned to the crucial issue in my own life: Love — or art. Was it a choice? I still wondered.

Deaths and Entrances, designed by Noguchi and scored by Hunter Johnson, probed the lives of three women authors: the Bronte sisters, Anne, Charlotte, and Emily. Especially intriguing to me was Emily Bronte, the wildest and most independent of the three sisters. How well I could identify with the restless, "different" and creative author of the classic novel, *Wuthering Heights*.

In this unusual piece, I cast myself as an author looking back over her life. The concept for this ballet was unusual and abstract, as I stretched myself into new artistic territory. My principle dancers personified my heroine's hopes and fears and passions, giving each emotion its own life through movement.

I took my audience inside the mind of Emily Bronte, who must choose between two opposing forces. One, danced by Erick Hawkins, was the *Dark Beloved*. The other, danced by Merce Cunningham, was the *Poetic Beloved*, a lighter being, almost a nature sprite — both dear to the conflicted heroine. Privately, I wondered about my casting.

Consciously, I did not see Erick as evil; quite the opposite. And yet the ballet portrayed the *Dark Beloved* as the Tempter, trying to lure the heroine away from her calling. Finally, Bronte found herself in a dilemma. Should she give herself to the dark being or the being of light? She agonized over the decision.

Who would win the heroine in the end?

A clear choice was expected. There was a twist instead. The heroine turned her back on both men, choosing rather a crystal goblet, symbolic of her lovely, lonely destiny as an artist. The reviews for *Deaths and Entrances* were mixed, but Merce and I won fine notices. Erick drew indifferent press or no notice at all. Once again he turned to his role of business manager.

~~~

"Indispensable?

This no longer seemed to be the right word for Erick Hawkins. Now he had made himself essential to the Graham studio. He demanded contracts. He arranged publicity. He approached patrons and pursued grants offered to the arts for the first time. *Am I entrusting him with too much?* I asked myself late at night. *Am I too dependent on him?*

I could not consult Louis, busy with his music and his young lover. I could guess what Agnes would say. But Erick's efforts were so diligent, I believed he was acting for my benefit and for the company. Otherwise, why would he work so hard for our collective welfare? Another inner voice countered with a more cynical approach:

Erick could control so much, he could take over.

He's learning how to manage any dance company.

A rival company. Or even a company of his own.

I refused to listen to that inner voice. I looked over the photos of myself with Erick at Bennington. Here was a couple caught up in a wild attraction and perhaps, a reckless passion. The pictures told more about these lovers than we ourselves could say.

There we were: heads thrown back as if we were drunk on wind. Stripped to the waist, Erick lifted me against his bare chest; my arms rose into the air as if in a spasm of joy. His face was tilted toward me and his gaze was consuming. Together, we seemed about to lift off from the earth and fly as a single airborne creature — for life, I hoped. For life.

~~~

A valentine without the frills.

A promise and a tribute.

A public declaration.

This was what I wanted to give Erick now. I had moved past the inner conflict shows in *Deaths and Entrances*. I was ready to show my commitment in a new creation: my most ambitious ballet. To the world I would declare myself through a lyrical American allegory. It would appear to be a simple story simply titled: *Appalachian Spring.*

A pioneer couple celebrated their wedding day and their new home on the frontier, attended by a preacher and a chorus of neighbors. The couple's love and union was my gift, through dance, to the man I loved. As I wrote this story out on my ancient typewriter; I moved from notes into narrative with ease, this time. Soon I had a synopsis. Now I had to find the right stage designer and the right composer to score my ballet.

The first quest was an easy one. Of course I would turn to my friend and sculptor Isamu Noguchi who grasped the new story as soon as I described it by phone. Isamu built models for the set — miniaturized so cleverly, each model could fit into a matchbox. He sent these from California to New York so I could imagine how we would work for a dance-drama.

"What do you think?" Isamu would ask.

"I need to mull it over," I would answer.

Before I could, a new model would arrive.

"I like it," I told Isamu at last. "It works! "

"You don't need to mull," he laughed. "You know."

"That's what you listen for. It's brilliant, Osamu."

"Now we can begin to try designs for the house."

It took time to translate a pioneer cabin into an abstract form; only a suggestion of a homestead conveyed with a few stark lines. Several matchboxes traveled across the country while I and Osamu worked out the visual backdrop and a set conducive to the dancers' movements.

Meanwhile, I wanted to commission an original score for the ballet. I sent the script to the brilliant composer, Aaron Copland. Instantly, he felt drawn to score my story. We, too, worked long-distance by correspondence. Aaron offered one suggestion for the script and I made several changes.

As the narrative came into focus, I waited with dwindling patience for Aaron's composition. It was unusual to set music to a ballet; it was almost an innovation then. Usually the music came first. For *Spring* the Graham/Copland method worked; that's what mattered.

At his piano, Aaron tried out different styles of American music. He favored the spare purity of an old Shaker hymn's melody, *Simple Gifts*.

This hymn ran through his score along with an early American folk dance, a Virginia Reel. Another theme conveyed the rugged exuberance of a rodeo. All these elements were woven into one symphonic composition. Aaron recorded himself playing this on his own piano and sent the record itself to me. When I heard it, I felt too stirred, too moved, to speak for several minutes. And I was touched by Aaron Copland's original title for the work: *"Ballet For Martha"*

As I searched for a different way to title the ballet, I came across a poem, once again, in my late-night process of writing and reading. It was a poem by Hart Crane and although it did not refer to the locale I had in mind, I liked the ring and spirit of it.

I was drawn to the word "spring," because it had three meanings, each conveying hope, life, and joy. I had made my decision. I would call my new work *Appalachian Spring*. Excited and exhausted all at once, I began to make the most important calls.

The first one was to Erick, who had played a major part behind the scenes. He had been the one to solicit and secure a grant to fund this project. Then I contacted Isamu and Aaron with my thanks and my congratulations. Everyone felt an unusual level of excitement about the work and its new title. I didn't sleep that night.

Now the hardest part began for me: the choreography. First I had to experiment and develop it. When all was done, I made a complete record of each step in my own form of dance notation — and, most important, what the movements meant. At the moment, that end process seemed so far away I couldn't quite imagine it.

Now, in my studio, I worked with my dancers, trying out sequences and movements that might tell the story in my mind. At first nothing seemed to turn out right. I imagined Isamu's frustration with his matchbox sets. Did he smash the failures? I would have. Growing frustrated myself, I took off my shoes and threw one against the wall. That released some of my creative tension but didn't carry me all the way through it.

Struggling, I let out a deep groan from the gut. Still no breakthrough, no relief. For me, the starting point of any dance was always a season of misery — and more than misery. Agony, I called it. No exaggeration. Even with support around me, I felt as if I were on a ship, alone, at sea. One of my students noted this struggle with alarm. She said I was a genius, and I always found an answer to creative problems. In the process, though, I got so intense, so frenetic, she thought I seemed to be "possessed."

My company stirred uneasily in the studio behind me. They went through this agony with me but this was the only way I knew how to work. For almost an hour I gazed out a window in the studio but I saw nothing of the street outside. Against the panes of glass I imagined myself into the time I wanted most: a wedding day.

This was what I had always asked of Louis, who could not, would not give it to me. Now I had another chance: Erick was open to the idea of marriage. I would tell him how I felt through this staged dance. Finally a sequence of movements began to emerge in my mind and in the studio. I turned from the window and as always, at this stage, I simply told my troupe, "Let's try this out."

~~~

And so it began.

There would be eight dancers, one bassoon, a flute, two cellos, one piano, four violins, one clarinet. There would be a stark set made of four crossed beams like the framework of a giant four poster bed. I had asked Osamu to design a rocking chair for the porch of the abstract cabin for the newlyweds. It was *the* chair I had visualized from the beginning.

As I moved to the music, more choreography came to me: a chorus of Puritan women, the movements of a square dance for bride and groom, joyous leaps; reflective pauses. And there would be simple period costumes: denims, chambray and, for the chorus, plain white bonnets. The color composition was like a bright April morning: a pattern of sky and a few clouds; a season of growth and hope.

In the completed ballet I tried to universalize the hopes of any couple, anywhere, starting a new life together. As always, in my work, there was a sense of ritual about the wedding and its celebration: joyous, optimistic, and eternal. The ballet ended in quiet simplicity. The new bride took her seat in the rocking chair and the groom stood behind her, resting one of his hands on her shoulder. This small gesture became large as the new couple seemed to blend and merge into one figure.

Danced by Erick and me, the ballet was infused with my deepest feelings; a genuine love, a private bond made public at last. *Appalachian Spring* premiered in Washington, D.C., on October 30, 1944, at the theatre of an imposing venue: The Library of Congress. An immediate and resounding success, the ballet was an instant American classic, compared to Thornton Wilder's *Our Town.* I could not express my relief and gratitude through words, through tears, even through movement.

John Martin, writing in *The New York Times,* saw *Appalachian Spring* as uplifting; a lyrical piece, infused with a special joy he had never seen before in my work: the dance of a young girl, he added. That review had intense meaning for me. At fifty, I could still be a convincing bride.

At thirty-five, Erick seemed to be a man of twenty-one, also filled with confidence and hope. Agnes de Mille, delighting in her good friend's success, recognized the work as a love letter. Aaron Copland won the Pulitzer Prize for his brilliant orchestral score, but the concept, book, and choreography were my own creation.

Now I hoped *Appalachian Spring* would play out in my life. This was my prayer, my driving goal, my dearest wish. True, Erick's reviews were bland compared with mine. True, I appeared to be the star of *Spring* while he seemed to be in a supporting role. Not to me, I insisted.

I saw Erick as the ballet's center. His spirits seemed to rise with my continued praise. We had made it together, as a team, I told him — at last he smiled to please me. There was something strained about the expression on his handsome face. How long could a forced smile last?

Friends seemed worried — but no one dared to make ominous predictions to me now. That would be mean-spirited, even cruel. We all watched and waited, as Erick created his first original ballet, a solo for himself, based on the rebellious and violent Abolitionist, John Brown.

From the start, this was a topic lacking audience appeal. Even so, I spent thousands of dollars to give a Erick's debut a flawless production, sparing no expense for sets, costumes, and music. Erick labored over the complex choreography. *John Brown* had to be right. Erick needed his own singular success. During the rehearsals and the premiere, I thought my nerves were worse than they were before my own performances.

John Brown opened to a "cold house," an unresponsive audience, and after it was over Erick locked himself in his dressing room — alone. I paced in the theatre until the first editions of the newspapers were out and reviews came in. The critics offered not one glimmer of praise. They panned the new ballet from concept to execution. *John Brown* was a public failure. Devastated, I rushed to Erick's dressing room. The door stood wide open. Newspapers were strewn across the floor. The place was empty.

On his own, Erick walked the streets all night. I never knew where he went or whom he might have seen. Most likely, I guessed, he had tramped about alone. When he returned home the next morning, I was in a frenzy of worry and tears. Shaking off my hands, he would not speak to me.

In strained silence, we opened the studio and started the day's first class. Still there were no words between us. There was no comment from the company. The classes went on, the routine was followed. But the Graham troupe felt the studio's air tightening around it. Erick spoke one sentence that day. He spat the words out. "I *will not be Mr. Graham.*"

Everyone had seen this coming.

Everyone except me.

∎

CHAPTER EIGHT

A thief, I called myself; a thief without shame.

I robbed from the rich, I added, from Picasso to Plato, and distributed their treasures, transformed, to others as their rightful legacy. I used this metaphor in lectures to explain the richness of my sources — and now I was tapping into one of the richest of all: Shakespeare.

This work was to be a star vehicle for the man I loved, and with his help, I struggled with the ballet's choreography. It had to be good. Great. Glorious. This might be my last chance to launch Erick into stardom and I knew it. A dancer gets a limited num-ber of attempts to make a breakthrough. Unfair, I thought, but a fact.

After one too many tries, the press always turned weary and dismissive. I could not let this happen, I told Noguchi on my office phone, as Erick burst in without knocking. For a moment, he stood over my desk, scanning the green baize blotter, a crystal bud vase, a fountain pen, a stack of mail. He lifted the bud vase and weighed it in his palm like a revolver. Finally he raised his voice.

"I'll make it, Martha. On my own."

I stood behind my desk. "Of course you will."

"Damn right." He tossed the vase into the air.

"No one ever said you wouldn't, darling."

"I'll hit the top." Another upward toss.

"And I'll be proud, Erick. I'm here to help."

"I'll do it *myself*." He caught the vase. "Watch."

"I will. I'll be right there. I believe in you."

"You believe in *you*." The vase glowed in his hand.

"That's not fair. You've *seen* me struggling."

Erick tossed the vase again. "I. Am. Not. You."

"Darling." I watched the falling vase. "I know."

"*Do* you?" He let the crystal shatter on the floor.

"Erick!" I rose as he slammed out of the room.

"It's messy," he called. "When things break."

Sighing, I went into the studio to teach class.

~~~

Martha plus Erick equaled war.

Erick plus Martha equaled joy.

Daily, the equation varied.

Our words were curt and few. Working, waking, dining, we could feel it: a taut silence stretched between us like a tightrope. Late at night, and only then, did that silence change. In bed, I would turn to him; reach for him. Erick would seize me and pull me close.

Abruptly, then, our tension would transform itself into fierce and furious lovemaking. We were equals then, one person; no doubts, no divisions. This shared passion was untouched by ordinary life, its choices and its conflicts. Engrossed in physical coupling, we always found a secret center, invisible to anyone else. Our salvation lay in each other, we agreed.

We traveled to our sanctuary: Santa Fe, New Mexico. As soon as we arrived, we went to our lean-to cabin. In a grove of aspen trees, shimmering, pale gold, the cabin sheltered us through four blue-sky days, three starlit nights. Our lovemaking was frequent, intense, almost ferocious. We could not seem to get enough of each other, even as we rested in each other's arms.

One noontide, after a morning of intimacy, the world seemed hushed; the birds went still. In the quiet, I whispered a hesitant admission: I needed Erick. He had needs, too, he said. And he knew how to get what we both were after. I assumed our longings were identical. I thought he must be saying his need for my love equaled his. So I hoped and so I heard his words. *I know how to get what we're both after.* There seemed only one thing left to do.

We rose. We packed. We drove. The old adobe town of Santa Fe was not far away. Its adobe piazza, flowering with hibiscus, seemed to welcome us. Indian craftsmen sat together at one end. Erick bought a turquoise ring for me; then, at the courthouse, we applied for a marriage license.

When I filled out the required forms, I took ten years off my age and wrote in "44". Erick, thirty-nine, noticed but said nothing. We made the simplest of arrangements. An early morning ceremony: private, Presbyterian. Two witnesses, one of them the organist. A short veil over my face. A single hibiscus blossom in my hand.

As I made my vows, I could not see my bridegroom's face but I hoped it was as flushed as mine. His voice was almost inaudible; his hands seemed to tremble for a moment. I pressed his cold fingers with mine. There was a pause after minister pronounced us "man and wife;" he reminded Erick to kiss the bride.

Looking back, I see that day in fragments: The blinding sun as Erick and I emerged from the dim church into the street. A handful of rice thrown by the organist. The smell of orange blossoms on the air. The wedding breakfast in the dining car of a train headed north to the Grand Canyon — and a brief honeymoon. Erick and I toasted each other with fresh-brewed coffee.

We had done it. *This is real,* I told myself. *Appalachian Spring* had played out in my own life after all, I thought, just when I was starting to give up. When Mr. and Mrs. Erick Hawkins returned to New York City, we phoned our announcement to everyone we knew. I wanted to send out embossed notes but these would take too long to print. The bride wanted this news to go out *now.*

It was received with polite restraint and frank surprise. Mrs. Rita Morgenthau, a close friend and supporter, threw a small party for us, "the newly-weds," in her elegant apartment. Another dear friend and patron, Mrs. Edith Isaacs was there, maternal as always, managing to mask her concern. Over champagne, caviar and cake, guests wished us well, but I heard how muted were the blessings. I told myself I didn't care, eventually our friends would see the rightness of this marriage.

And then we were back into the studio's routine, its classes and rehearsals, and the business of managing the company. Erick, as always, was successful with this ongoing effort. And now he was proud to disclose his biggest idea, already translated into bookings. With an expansive smile and broad gestures, Erick announced his latest plans for my company: Nationwide tours.

~~~

How could I say "No" to this? It would not be good for the dancers in terms of fitness, flexibility, and rehearsal time. Still, it would be good for the company's recognition, not to mention its finances. Erick should have consulted me, I well knew, but I let it go. He wanted my congratulations and he got them, along with a cactus, imported from Santa Fe. Then the company piled onto the buses, promoted as "Coaches" and each trip, as "A Ride On Air."

"If this is how it feels to ride on air, I'll row a boat," said Nan, the brash redheaded soloist. In fact, the "coaches" smelled like ancient armchairs, disinfectant, and occasionally, mildew. The rides were often jolting; Pepsi Cola shot from bottles, sandwiches flew into the aisle. You might skid when you stood up; you might land in someone's lap. On the bus, everyone tried to stretch and bend and stay limber; me included. Even so, routine movements turned into risky exploits in the swaying aisles.

"It's like dancing on a bowling ball," Merce said.

"It's like risking your ever-loving neck," said Nan.

"Is this worth it?" I asked Erick one evening.

"What the hell do you think?" He flared up at me.

"There are some complaints." I held my ground.

Erick thrust written facts and figures in my face. The traveling paid off in crucial ways, he said; his favorite combination — Fame and Funds. The itinerary was continually enlarging. More and more towns and cities issued invitations to the troupe. The Martha Graham Dance Company was increasingly in demand. Erick's swagger grew more than a bit.

Successful as we were, these tours were exhausting, especially when a single performance was flanked by day-long traveling. There was so much unpacking and repacking for everyone. There was contraction and release, flexion and extension — in the seats or outside, at stops.

I was always quiet on the bus, often reading or scribbling in my notebooks. Erick seldom sat with me. He seldom sat at all. The man's restless energy never burned off. The company watched him pace the bus from end to end, watching everyone and everything. I seemed a world away; I put myself there on purpose. Eric often tested my nerves and patience with his roaming. Trying to be friendly, he told stories of his time with the great Balanchine's company, although Eric never mentioned his disappointments there.

"We had a ballet featuring a wild Denishawn orgy," Erick told everyone. "The principle soloist had a problem with her costume. It came loose at the top, drooping lower, lower, lower. Well, what do you think happened?"

"Do tell," said Nan. "You have a captive audience."

"Well, she hissed for help toward the end. I heard her and I solved her problem. I ripped off her top. Well, it was supposed to be an orgy."

The company's female contingent did not find this story funny in the least. Cautionary mental notes were made: *Don't let Erick get too close on stage.* I could sense these thoughts before I heard the whispers. I winced at this story and Erick gave me a black look. We whispered at the front of the bus:

"Who are you to judge my taste in jokes?" he hissed.

"I'm not judging you at all." My voice was frosty.

"I'm your husband now. Remember your vows?"

"I promised 'To love, honor and cherish.'"

"I heard the minister use the word 'Obey.'"

To dodge an argument, I laughed that off.

The tour pressed on to San Francisco; everyone exclaimed over the Golden Gate Bridge. Erick, charmed by the hilly city, walked its sloping streets and turned up late for a company rehearsal. It was my turn to send a black look, but I managed to control myself — to everyone's surprise. Was I giving in or giving up? I asked myself. I was too weary just now for confrontation.

I finished the run-through and returned to my room without a word to Erick. I had learned how sensitive his ego was; reprimands only caused more strain, more tension, more public quarrels. These, I knew, were bad for company morale. And for these, I was as much to blame as he.

I would wait to find the right time for another "discussion." This was still my company; I was still its director. And this time I would not throw a shoe across the room. "That might disturb the roaches," I muttered. We were moving into yet another boarding house with creaky beds and creaky floorboards.

To work off my anger, I ironed the entire company's linen that afternoon. I would spread a shirt over the back of an armchair, add some starch and go at it, as I'd done in my old walk-up flat. Now, dancers drifted into my room to chat, drawn by the familiar smell of hot starched linen and the sight of me in a domestic role. With my hair tied back, my sleeves rolled up, I joked with everyone around me.

"Blindfold me, girls, before I do the gents' undies."

"Their leotards show more," Nan winked.

"We don't notice anyone's...equipment."

"*Equipment.*" Genial laughter. "That's new."

"Old as time, my dears," I told them.

More laughter. A box of chocolates made the rounds. I sprinkled starch on one of the men's shirts and applied the iron to the broadcloth.

"Will someone scratch my nose please?" I asked.

"Wouldn't want you scorching our shirts. There."

"Grand. Done." I took a bow to my company's applause. There were more chocolates, more laughs, and an easygoing buzz while Erick stood aloof in the doorway, looking on.

~~~

When the company returned to its New York base, I sat down with Erick and a man representing Sol Hurok. *The* Sol Hurok. *The* famed theatrical producer and impresario. He was interested in doing publicity for the "Graham outfit," well-established now, with a wide following — big enough to attract a seasoned pro like Hurok. Erick, naturally, had set this situation up and he was flexing his authoritative muscles.

From the start, he took control of the meeting. Before I could get past my greeting, Erick was directing the session. Before any discussion, he said he had certain central terms to lay out — stunning terms: Equality with me; equal program notes; equal number of solos.

I stared at Erick. Defiant, he stared back at me.

"I'm your partner. *And* your husband."

I know how we can get what we're both after.

I heard these words again; now in a different way.

"You've been planning for this, Erick," I said.

"Who wouldn't? I don't act without thinking."

"Nor do I." I sighed. "Except with you."

"I think that's an insult, not a compliment."

"You're not the groom you were in Santa Fe."

"And you're not forty-four," he shot back.

Sensing trouble, the theatre "rep" acted quickly. A long distance call was placed directly to Hurok himself. His emissary fixed Erick and me with a look and stated one simple fact: If we did this deal, what *Hurok* said went. No one else. After all, the man ran one of the largest theatrical management firms in the world.

It was an honor to merit his attention and consideration. Enough said?

The call went through: four rings.

In a cold fury, I sat completely still. I heard Erick's demands repeated and I felt slapped twice over. Slapped and betrayed. The representative talked on. At last, Sol Hurok's voice boomed through the phone into the quiet office. He gave his professional opinion and he gave it in his own blunt style:

"The Graham name sells tickets — the Hawkins name isn't worth a damn. Graham sells — got it?" With that the impresario hung up.

Erick went red. "Put me on the line right now."

"Too late, I'm afraid, Mr. Hawkins. He's gone."

For a moment, I could taste Erick's humiliation.

"We'll see." I told the rep. "Thanks for your time."

"Anyone would jump at this," Hurok's man told us.

"We only jump in the studio," I said. "Good day."

After he'd gone, Erick spat harsh words:

"I told you, 'I will not be Mr. Martha Graham.' "

I waited until I could turn my voice to cold steel:

"You manage this company — not me."

I rose, left the office and retreated to my dressing room. This was always my sanctuary in times of conflict, crisis, or inner turmoil. Here I kept my notebooks now; here I could think — behind a locked door.

It took me several moments before I could stop myself from shaking. It was rage that made me tremble now, not fear. Looking in the mirror, I remembered what I'd told my troupe of girls about the cost of dancing. *That has to be the center of your lives. Even if it means losing a lover or a husband,* I had said. *Your art is your life.*

Now, in my dim dressing room, these words seemed to mock me. Did I still believe in them? Once I had called myself "doom-eager." Was I still? *Whatever the cost, it was your destiny and you had to do it.* I remembered saying that. It seemed a long time ago. I was younger then, much younger: a girl ignorant of sexual passion and deep romantic love. What had I known at twenty-two?

Now I was a woman of fifty-six, however young I still appeared. The choices were no longer easy.

Should I sacrifice my own artistic level to let my husband shine? Didn't marriage, too, demand my all? For a long while I sat alone in the dusky room and listened to the sounds rising from the street beyond. A dog's bark. A child's cry. The screech of brakes, the beep of horns. Real life, so close, so attainable, but perhaps, not for me. *I hate show business cliches,* I thought. *Isn't this the classic battle? Can a man stand second billing? Can this man?*

Daylight began to fade around me. The face in the mirror seemed to fade as well. I snapped on my dressing table lamps. The room sprang back into focus.

~~~

There might be a solution to this dilemma — if only I could reach it through the medium of dance I would write a ballet focused on a strong male character. I'd had my own successful run of mythic Greek heroines: Medea, Jocasta, Ariadne. I had tried to feature Erick in another dance: *Errand Into the Maze*. It focused on the fearsome Minotaur, a legendary creature, dwelling underground in a labyrinth. For centuries the Minotaur held sway, but at last the heroine, Ariadne, confronts and slays the monster. That was my version.

This dance-drama had won critical acclaim as an expression of the human struggle with repressed savagery and darkness. Even so, I had been unwise in my casting choice with *Errand*. I had substituted Erick for the original dancer in the Minotaur role. As powerful as it was, Erick did not like playing the villain; especially a defeated one. I saw my mistake, too late. *As always*, I added.

This time I would not "steal" from Plato or Homer, Dickinson or Bronte. I would go to the master, William Shakespeare, and his most redemptive tragedy: *King Lear*. In the complex role of the king himself, Erick would be centerstage at last. Make-up could easily transform him into the aging monarch, passing from foolishness to wisdom, arrogance to humility.

Was this my hidden wish for Erick, I wondered, in life as well as art? For now, I brushed that vexing question to one side. This ballet had already started to consume me.

To this ballet I would give my all: my art, my knowhow, my experience. It would be a star vehicle for Erick. No villains like Macbeth for him, no jealous leaders like Othello. Nothing too complex, like *Hamlet.* How rich it could be — Lear's movement through the storm around him and the storm within him. The way suffering leads the character to know himself, admit his flaws, and reconcile with his loyal daughter, Cordelia.

I was already writing in my notebook. A title for the piece came right away. Usually it took me a long time to name a work. *A good omen,* I thought. Lear and Shakespeare would surely launch Erick as a star in his own right.

The Eye of Anguish, starring Erick Hawkins, opened on a January night at the Forty-sixth Street Theatre in New York. Despite all the efforts that went into it, both Erick and the ballet drew bad press and a cold audience reaction. The role of Lear was too deep and broad for the soloist. Erick could not imagine himself into the aging monarch's skin. Lear's dawning humility escaped Erick; he could not dance the part with assurance.

The ballet's reviews were pans, without exception, including *The New York Times.* I saw, too late, how Erick failed to inhabit and express this great role. It wasn't merely Erick's age or maturity. The press was critical of his prowess. Even my choreography received mixed reviews, though rumors flew that Erick himself had tinkered with the work.

Whatever happened, he was too devastated to hide his feelings. Before that premiere, he had anticipated the success and praise he'd craved for years. Long before, when Balanchine refused to gave him solo parts, there was still time to recoup. Now time had grown short. Erick was nearing a vulnerable age for dancers. And at this point, he still had failed to make it.

After a long silence, Erick slammed out of the theatre and disappeared into the night. As he did after the *John Brown* fiasco, he walked the streets until the sky began to lighten in the East.

■

CHAPTER NINE

"Where did you go?"

"Nowhere, really."

"What did you do?"

"Nothing much."

How many of our conversations went like that, I wondered, after Erick's sudden, unexplained return? He did not reek of alcohol or perfume — only sweat. I believed he did walk the streets for hours. I knew his restless energy and his flash-fire reaction to rejection. He had never quite recovered from Balanchine's coldness. "Mr. B." had never offered Erick a solo, so Erick quit the company. Here he had too much invested. He would have to find another way to make his breakthrough now.

If only he could glory in his talent for business and focus on that. But Erick wanted more. He drove himself to be my match — but nothing I could do would make him so. Nor could Erick admit his own weaknesses; it was easier for him to blame me and my choreography. And blame me he did.

"You tried to undercut me, Martha."

"Of course not, why would I do that?"

"You have to star. You gave me bad material."

"Erick, that's ridiculous, I tried my best for you."

"Of course, you can't admit to being wrong."

"Can you? You had nothing to do with this?"

"*You're* accusing *me*?" He slapped my face.

"How dare you?" I slapped his hand away.

"I'm your husband, Martha. Do you hear me?"

"I do. The whole damn company hears you."

"Fine with me. I'm its manager, remember?"

I said nothing, fearing he'd walk out again. I was keeping secrets from him now: Pain in my soul, pain in my gut, and, most worrisome, pain in my knee. There was no time for escape or injury just now. This time we could not run off to Santa Fe. We must use every moment to prepare for an event that overshadowed

Erick's failure. Soon we would lead the troupe on a European tour — a first for the Graham company.

~~~

Erick took control once more. When I suggested working together on the Paris/London program he was curt. The program was already set, he told me. Erick had it all arranged with Craig Barton, my secretary. Now Erick looked up, taunting me with his grin, daring me to speak one word of protest. I did.

"It's set? Without consulting me — at all?"

"You were absorbed in rehearsals," he dodged.

"Show me the program, Erick. That's my right."

"Why didn't you ask before?" He passed it to me.

For a long moment, I stared at the paper in my hand. The program's centerpiece was *The Eye of Anguish*, starring Erick Hawkins.

"You want to destroy this company?" I demanded.

"You want to destroy your husband's last chance?"

"I have the right to finalize the program, Erick."

"The program," he grinned, "has gone to press."

"Reprint it, Erick." I was furious but firm.

"Too late." Again, that grin. "It's been released."

"Released?" My voice began to rise. "*Where?*"

"To the press corps. In Paris and, yes, London."

"*How dare you?*" I wanted to shake him.

"Why not? I *am* this company's manager."

"But not *my* manager." I spat. "I told you that."

"Is this a little menopausal moment? Dah-ling?"

"Go to hell." I could no longer control my voice.

"*I'm already there,*" he shouted. "*You sent me.*"

It was the end of the day. The dancers were already leaving the studio and going down the stairs. Outside, they must have heard our raised voices, even with the windows closed. Uneasy, Gert Macy, the office manager, came back in. The fight had worsened in the office where it had begun. Both of us were still shouting. Erick had pinned me flat against a wall, holding my arms fast, while I kicked out with bare feet.

Spitting, fuming, I struggled to free myself; he wrestled me back against the wall. As we grappled with each other, I loosened Erick's grip. He grabbed me — and then I was crashing down on my weak knee, crying out as I hit the floor. It happened so fast, I'm still not sure who did what. He threw me down, I thought. He always said I fell.

We stood there yelling accusations. It was ugly, it was vicious, it was marriage at its worst. Somehow Gert pulled us apart and led me into another room. Grimacing in pain, I could hardly walk away. I had one week to heal before the company sailed for Paris.

A nightmare of a week, that's what it was. Now on crutches, I continued to conduct rehearsals. Erick did not speak to me, even after I had medical treatment. He seemed to feel justified about "the accident." Rumors spread and they reached me. Such a tight community was sure to comment on this inhouse drama. Some said it was all my fault; I had sabotaged the tour. I did not want my husband to shine in *The Eye of Anguish*. The irony of this title was not lost on anyone.

These rumors were difficult to believe. No dancer would sabotage her own body. Nor would I sabotage my company's chances for a glorious European tour. I knew the welcome Bethsabee de Rothschild had prepared for us in Paris. How could I disappoint her and my dancers? Most of all, this company was my child, my creation, my concern. Everybody who belonged to it knew this. After twenty-four hours, all whispers stopped. I didn't want to know the source of such malicious rumors.

The relentless grind of back-to-back rehearsals continued eight hours a day. I forced myself to strengthen my muscles without risking my knee. I felt the intense scrutiny of company members — a mix of genuine concern and genuine fear. Would I be able to dance? Could I?

Each day I was scanned for signs of progress. No one wanted the tour to be cancelled now. With two days to go, I switched from crutches to a cane. This was taken as a hopeful sign. I was counting on the strength of my own will. If I could electrify a room with just one glance, surely I could tell my body what to do.

Leery of more injuries, every member of the troupe stayed focused on safety as well as artistry. Now and then a thrill passed through the studio, usually on breaks, when the international debut was discussed. This was an extraordinary opportunity and everyone knew it. London gleamed in the distance. In the foreground, Paris waited, like a glimmering mirage.

And not just any mirage.

Bethsabee's mother, the Baroness herself, was welcoming me, her daughter's friend, with my entire troupe, to stay at the two-hundred-year old Rothschild mansion on the Rue St. Honore. A few hours after the dancers settled in, we would be the guests of honor at that famous landmark, the elegant Plaza-Athenee Hotel.

There the Baroness de Rothschild herself would host a champagne reception for her guests, as well as press, peers, patrons of the arts — all to honor me and America's foremost modern dance company. *Tout-Paris* would attend this gala welcome; it would be *the* event of the year's social season. A new decade was beginning with our introduction to Europe.

At last it was time for what seemed to be the most excellent of all adventures. All of it sounded like a fairy tale to me, to all of us — complete with a princess and a castle. I never had enough words of thanks for

Bethsabee and the generosity of the Baroness de Rothschild. Even if it only lasted for a day, this would be a gift no one could forget.

The Graham troupe began to board a transatlantic steamer at New York City's Chelsea piers. Well-wishers were waving from the shore; the ship was strewn with pennants, ribbons, and confetti. Once on deck, excitement seized the company. Champagne corks and cameras were popping. A dancer cartwheeled across the deck. Fellow travelers applauded. I watched from one end of the rail; Erick watched from the other. It was all a blur to me, even looking back. Nothing could dull my nerves; aspirin dulled the pain in my knee.

I gazed over at Erick's stony face.

How happy we should be, I thought.

How miserable we are, I saw.

Over and over, I told myself, all would be well once we get to Paris. But I found it hard to hear that inner hopeful voice. Instead, there was one persistent question running through my mind:

How will I get through this?

~~~

I got through it on aspirin, adrenalin, and anger.

An admiring French press covered the Rothschild reception at the Hotel Plaza-Athenee. There were hundreds of coral-colored roses in enormous porcelain pots in the lobby and throughout the ballroom. There were yards and yards of Persian rugs. Velvet draperies. Gilded chairs. Antique tables. The grand hotel formed the perfect backdrop for a cultural gala, replete with powerful and prestigious guests. The expectations seemed impossible to meet. Somehow, and I still don't know how, I did not disappoint Bethsabee or her mother.

My hair was drawn back into a chignon at the nape of my neck. I wore a simple white silk gown with a crimson wrap, bordered in midnight blue. Admiring comments followed me and my ensemble — it was a subtle echo of both countries' flags, as I had designed it to be.

That evening, my dancers were slightly dazed, slightly giddy, fizzy, awed. They seemed proud to be there. They seemed proud to be with me. I was a cross between a princess and a panther, someone said. Erick turned away.

Swallowing more aspirin, I mingled with the guests and won praise from the French press. Bethsabee greeted the entire company with warmth, as did her elegant mother. The Baroness had memorized every dancer's picture and greeted each of them by name.

Erick stood back, saying little, and refused champagne. The next day he was not mentioned in the papers. There was no time to pore over who said what of whom, however. Opening night was almost upon the troupe. It went into a fever of final rehearsals.

To the dancers' horror, the stage was raked: not flat but slanted, as many European stages are. It took extra hours to find sure footing and learn how to keep balanced. Erick seemed distressed. He practiced hard, trying to compensate for the raked surface; all the while he was anticipating his European solo. His great chance. His international debut. Curtain time was hours away, as was his breakthrough.

The house was sold out, packed with persons of importance, personally invited by the Baroness de Rothschild and her daughter, Bethsabee. The guest list included such luminaries as the Countess of Noailles, a generous supporter of the arts; a famed couturier; the composer Poulenc, and other notables.

Pacing, trembling, I was too overwrought to lend enough support to my company. The pressure on each dancer seemed almost unbearable. How do you follow such a buildup, so many exalted expectations? Even the First Lady, Mrs. Eleanor Roosevelt was expected to take a seat of honor in a central first-tier box with a perfect view of the stage.

But where *was* Mrs. Roosevelt?

At curtain time her box was empty.

Last minute word came in by telephone

The First Lady's car was moments away.

The producers' huddle reached a decision:

"Hold the curtain," the stage manager called.

"Don't hold it for that woman," Erick shouted.

The producers stared at him. " *'That woman?'* "

"Or any woman!" he said. "Start without her."

The house lights dimmed. Backstage the dancers finished stretching and gripped each others' cold hands. Slowly, with great majesty, the curtain rose. The first piece, *Errand Into the Maze,* was danced by Erick and me. Our hostility actually lent an edge to our performance, but the chemistry was off and the piece was all wrong for the audience.

I struggled to contain my fury over Erick's choice of opener. As I expected, it met with a tepid response from the glittering spectators. The entire first act unfolded that same way. The programming was not right for Paris and not in keeping with the gala's festive mood.

Intermission brought a new confrontation. Erick rushed over to Craig Barton, my secretary, and ordered him to forbid the use of cameras by the audience. Craig refused this time; inadvertently, he used the wrong words: "How could anyone have the nerve to command dignitaries from around the world, *here to honor Martha?*"

Erick, in a rage, could not shake this off — and his performance would open the second act of the production in only a few minutes. If he could not succeed here and now, I wondered what would happen.

Once again, the footlights glowed, the house lights dimmed, and the curtain rose on *The Eye of Anguish*, Erick's self-chosen star vehicle. Still angered by Craig's comment, Erick stomped on stage. Lear's progress toward humility was lost before it even began. The performance drew only silence, punctuated by some scattered booing.

Trembling with anger, Erick finally made his exit into the wings. He tried to save face, likening his reception to the riot caused by Nijinsky when he danced a new work in Paris. Of course, in this case, there had been no riot. Nor was Erick a Nijinsky. He retreated to his dressing room.

I took the stage next in *Medea*, yet another Greek tragedy, dark and heavy, and also the wrong choice for Paris. It was the wrong choice for me as well, that night, since it put stress on my knees. The raked stage added extra challenges. Instead of adjusting the choreography, I went through every perilous position as I tried to salvage the entire show.

The program closed with my comedic ballet, *Every Soul Is A Circus* which came too late in the evening. It should had been the opener, I knew, a way to engage the audience; now everyone was too tired now to care. I danced with quiet humor but I clenched my teeth; I was churning inside. There was nothing quiet about Erick's rage. It showed in each movement he made and finally, it seemed, he took his anger out on me, his partner.

In the wings, one of our best male dancers, watched the *pas de deux* with horror. He had no jealousy of Erick, no reason to lie when he gave his post-performance report: Erick raised me too high during a *jetté*, a jumping lift, and let me down too hard, too fast — on my wounded knee. The shock caused my leg to collapse beneath me and I might had fallen. I barely made it offstage.

The evening ended with yet another long reception at the Rothschild mansion and Erick stormed off to our room. Soon I joined him but I was too fretful and overtired to sleep. Pacing in the room's foyer, I was awake much of the night, anticipating dawn and the incoming reviews. As expected, they were flat, confused, and for the most part, unfavorable. There were some dissenting opinions, praising me. Set up as the star, Erick was ignored.

And now he must carry the show, with backup from its principles. Injured again, I had to admit I could not dance. Raging in the wings through the second night's performance, I watched my company begin to flounder. The press spread word of the star's injury. The public stop buying tickets. The Paris run was terminated. Much of the company was in tears. I tried to rally them. We still had another chance — we still had London.

~~~

Across the channel, in a Bloomsbury hotel, the shaken company tried hard to regroup. Before rehearsals could begin, John Martin called from *The New York Times*. His call was not official; he made it as a friend. John's voice was urgent. If I could not dance, the company *must* cancel. He was adamant. A bad run was far worse than no run at all. After the French fiasco the company had to cut its losses. There was regretful agreement.

But I knew what would happen next. I realized how strongly Eric would resent advice. No one told him what to do, especially a critic. As I expected, Erick decreed the show would go on as planned. And I decided, unwisely, I would dance.

London was expecting to see me in performance. I had to go on. I felt compelled to do something, anything, to redeem this tour. With my knee braced and packed in ice, I awaited the next day's dress rehearsal. The premiere would follow the rehearsal after little more than an hour to stretch, to breathe, to touch up makeup. The night before, I did two things:

I had a car drive me to the theatre so I could check the stage. Thank God, I thought: It wasn't raked. Then, still limping, I asked the driver to take me to a church, any church that was open. There I lit three candles: one for the company, one for my marriage, and one for my knee.

After stretching and flexing exercises in the morning, the dress rehearsal finally began. This program opened with *Appalachian Spring,* my valentine to

Erick. We would dance the roles of the newlyweds, as we did on that triumphant night, six years before. During dress rehearsal, I forced myself through demanding bent-knee swoops and jump-lifts with Erick, who had to take care how he set me down.

Perhaps my injury hampered me and threw off my timing. Perhaps Erick failed me once again as he seemed to do in Paris. However it happened, I came down from another *jette* too hard on the injured knee. I tried to rally but I could not force my body to move beyond its limits now. Even with my strength of will, I was defeated. I could not dance in the premiere. The dress rehearsal ended in disaster.

Our tour could not succeed without me, Erick knew. But this was his moment. If American audiences refused to accept him, he must make his name abroad. He insisted that the tour go on. We argued — no, we fought. We cursed each other, struggling for control. Why had I given Erick so much power? Too late now, he said. I tried to shake him; he, in turn, shook me off.

"I'm your equal," he spat. "You can't stand that."

"You want to take over, Erick? Do it all?"

"Why not? You can't dance. I'll run the tour."

"Oh no, Erick. This is still *my* company."

"I refuse to give up London, it's important."

"The tour is not *your* personal showcase."

"You've held me back too long — I'm leaving."

"My God." I stared at Erick. "You can't do that."

"Can't I? I'll make it on my own, I told you."

"You'll regret it, Erick — quitting like this."

"No. I'll be relieved. No more of your bitchery."

"You're cruel, you're devious. I always knew it."

"Go on, call names, Martha. I don't give a damn."

"I wonder if you ever really did," I said quietly.

I went into the bathroom and threw cold water on my face. Without looking in the mirror, I knew my eyes were red and swollen. Leaning over the sink, I took deep breaths. *One...and two...*The counting and the running water seemed to calm me.

Perhaps if I were gentle, not angry; loving, not combative, I could forge some kind of peace. *It can't end like this*, I told myself. *I can't let it go this way. I won't.* I smoothed my hair, dried my face, and opened the door. There was an odd silence. I paused, listening. Then I moved toward the bedroom.

Erick was gone.

His armoire and his drawers were empty.

On the table lay two coins beside a note. Shaking, I opened it and read: *"Left you & Co. Won't ever be back. Erick."*

After ten years, a note and two shillings.

I could not find anything else.

I sat down at the dressing table. This, I knew, was not like the other times when Erick walked the streets all night. He had never taken his things away; he had never left a note. He had never spoken to me as he did tonight. My young husband had dropped me flat.

Now he would go on without me, as he'd warned me, and try to make it on his own. He would go back to America for a while, I thought. When I finally returned home, his clothes and pens and shaving soap — all his things would be gone from my flat and the studio. There would be no forwarding address.

Abruptly I felt chilled. I could not get warm, even in the feather bed, even under the down comforter. I glanced at the window, hidden by drawn curtains. Beyond them, at that moment, Erick was walking away from me into the dark. Despite myself, despite all reason, I hoped he might return. I felt like a child, clinging to a kite string, though the kite itself was lost.

Somewhere a clock chimed the hour. That was Big Ben, I realized, and this was London, a city I did not know. I seemed to look down on myself from a great height: Huddled on the bed, I was alone, injured, and far from home. My reputation was damaged; my company, as well. Somehow I must get my dancers through this thing. But how?

I had often compared dancers to trees. We bent, we swayed, we moved with the wind, we penetrated earth and sky. Now, for the first time, I felt no tree of life stirring within me. I doubted I could still reach down and draw up strength from my own roots. Perhaps they would no longer hold me fast in this new, uncertain soil.

I rolled from bed to the floor and pulled myself upright. A flash of pain shot through my knee but I forced myself to stay on my feet. Holding to the bed-post with one hand, I tried to find some word, some thought, some verse to get me through this night. For a while, I stood there, stiff and still. Then I recalled the message I gave my company at the end of every season — and surely, this season had ended.

I let the bedpost go. The pain grew worse, but I planted my feet on the thick pink carpet in the center of the room. In the silence I heard my own voice. It quavered at first, then grew firm and even.

"No matter what, I am still a dancer."

■

CHAPTER TEN

Brava, Martha! Brava!

Curtsies, roses, cheers, applause.

Home again, at Carnegie Hall.

It had taken me six long months to get there. After the London disaster, Bethsabee de Rothschild had rescued me and brought me to America to heal. Surgery for the injured knee had been highly recommended. Naturally, I had refused this advice. If I wanted to continue performing, I could not risk an operation. I would not take cortisone injections. My search for medical solutions ended there.

I was determined to heal myself. I would restore my body as dancers have a way of doing — and this I would accomplish on my own. First I fled to the clear-skied peace and quiet of New Mexico, where friends offered me one of their homes. Intense, as usual, I began to invent and improvise a program of my own exercises, designed to strengthen the bad knee and the leg.

Lift a twenty-five pound typewriter with an weakened leg? Crazy, friends told me. For God's sake, don't try it. Naturally, this became my ultimate goal during recovery. Of course, I had to work up to this feat; it took time and concentrated effort. I'd begun with stretches, then small weights, then larger ones. Slowly, my program had began to work. When I felt I was ready, I set myself the hardest test.

I put my typewriter inside a bag, tied the bag to my leg and with that leg I lifted the machine into the air. Twice a day, I forced myself to raise this heaviest of all my weights. By that time, I was certain: I would dance again. I began to make notes for another ballet and pushed myself to the choreography stage.

~~~

The new solo work was titled, *Judith.*

This was drawn from a story in the Biblical Apocrypha. The story centered on a Jewish heroine's most daring act; I had it read to me in Hebrew. The ballet showed another formidable woman striking out against oppression — Judith slew a cruel tyrant and liberated her own people. Clever and courageous, she perfumed and rouged myself, then put on jewels and silks.

When she entered the enemy camp, Judith, mistaken for a courtesan, slipped inside the royal tent. There she seduced the tyrant, plied him with strong drink, and when he weakened, Judith took his life. Her weapon was the evil man's own sword.

For good measure, Judith drove a nail through the tyrant's head. Then, without alarming any of the guards, she disappeared into the dark. Judith's safe return to her camp was a triumphant one; her story was told and retold. And there I was, retelling it again, this time, without words.

No questions were raised about the connection between spurned wife and avenging heroine. If people wondered whether one event provoked the other, they kept such speculations to themselves. To audiences who did not know my personal history, the ballet had the attraction of a universal theme: A victory for the underdog. In those post-war years, such motifs struck a strong nerve.

I was grateful and relieved at the ballet's success. If this comeback work had been rejected, I would have found that hard to bear. At the end of *Judith's* world premiere, the audience response was so sustained, so vocal, and so fervent it could be heard throughout the house, from the prop department to the ushers' lounge to the empty dressing room.

After the last curtain call, I retreated to my sanctuary, as I always did. Something near the mirror caught my eye; I broke into sudden tears. Startled, my friends asked what could have happened to distress me so. Just moments earlier, I had flashed my smile from center stage. What could have reduced me to tears after such a powerful performance — and such a prolonged standing ovation? Perhaps this was simply an outflow of relief and gratitude?.

Silent, still weeping, I showed them all a book of poetry carefully set out on the dressing table. During my performance someone had entered the room and placed the volume there. It lay open to a favorite verse, one I had read aloud with Erick at our most intimate of times. The poem was our secret; no one else could have known about it. Certainly no one else knew what deep emotions it would evoke from me.

Erick had been seen inside the theatre that night, the house manager happened to remember. My dressing room was always open. Erick must have placed the poem where I could not fail to miss it. The house manager had not been concerned. "How thoughtful," he said now. "He wanted to show his thoughts were with you."

Others were less certain. Didn't Erick Hawkins understand exactly how that verse would affect me? He knew me so well; he could gauge my emotional reactions. Erick had not yet found success; I had, once again. If he had wanted to make an impact on my night of triumph, he had certainly succeeded, whatever his intentions.

Opinions varied on Erick's motives but I was no longer listening. I sat stunned, wiping trails of mascara from my cheeks. Disgusted, a friend snatched the book from the table and laid it away in the prop room where it just might happen to get lost. I never saw that particular volume of poetry again. Nor did I search for it.

~~~

Meanwhile, telegrams were arriving at my dressing room. Corks flew. Glasses clinked. Vases filled. But the fragrance of three dozen long-stemmed roses could not lift the dark mood hanging in the air like smoke. My hard-earned comeback had been marred. The poem's abrupt appearance had peeled away my mask of self-reliance and recovery. I was far from healed.

Every night was the same. Alone, I could not sleep. Often I fled my flat, filled with reminders of Erick. I often found myself moving toward my empty studio. There I lay face down on the floor, weeping against the boards themselves; I hoped they might muffle my sobs. I could hear the sound of my own keening: it was the cry of a wounded animal, a beast in agonizing pain. My body shook, my fingernails scraped the wood beneath my groping hands.

I had not mourned like this since my brother's death, almost fifty years before. Now there was no open field to absorb my pain, no fatherly presence to offer comfort. There was only this room, this floor. This movement. It was reminiscent of my early ballet, *Lamentation.* No matter how Erick had wounded me, I still cared for him. This was a love beyond reason, I knew; beyond explanation. Male companionship was still welcome to me, but no man would ever capture me entirely as Erick had. That ecstatic self-abandonment was over for me. And for this loss, too, I grieved.

One night, hoping to work late, a Graham dancer slipped into the darkened, empty studio. John Butler thought he was alone. Pausing in the dimness, he heard the wrenching cry of something not quite human. Without turning on the lights, John scanned the space ahead of him. He hesitated, then drew nearer. Embarrassed, I sensed his approach.

"Martha?" John Butler whispered. "Is that you?"

Startled, I moved reflexively, still weeping, trembling all over. Shocked and worried, John stayed with me until my spasms of grief began to ease. As we left, we stepped over a program dropped near the studio door. It was a Carnegie Hall program, featuring my newest solo. I must have been too distraught to notice it had fallen, or I was simply too miserable to care. John knew me well and understood the source of my pain; I did not have to tell him what was wrong.

"Is it very late?" my voice was ragged.

"Very." He bent over me. "Let me take you home."

"Oh, I'm so sorry, John. What a mess I am."

"No need to be sorry. Take my hand."

~~~

Kind and courtly, John Butler walked the streets with me for hours that night and many others. When the sky began to lighten, he walked me to my flat. I thanked him once again. "My privilege," he said. And meant it. John had seen me at my worst, my most disheveled. Now I felt no shame in turning to him, a man just over thirty, young enough to be my son. To my surprise, John seemed quietly delighted to be my friend.

He talked with me as we wandered the twisting streets of Greenwich Village late at night. We passed the shuttered shops, the outdoor cafes, the dog-walkers and other wanderers, perhaps insomniacs like me. To distract me, John turned the subject to himself. Growing up in Greenville, Mississippi, John was raised to be chivalrous with women. It was, for me, a refreshing trait.

In his Mississippi drawl, John tried to speak of ordinary life and ordinary memories. The soft sweet air at home. The loneliness of an only child with a vivid imagination. Tall and handsome, John's first job was modeling men's suits in a department store. This wasn't quite what his parents had in mind for their son. Nor was it quite what John had in mind for his own future, even when his different path ruptured his close family.

"Dad wanted an education for me," he told me.

"Did you come up North to go to a university?"

He smiled. "I came because I knew I had to dance."

"It was the same for me. Did your parents help?"

"Not quite," John sighed. "Dad cut me off."

"I'm sorry. What made you so sure, so young?"

"A woman." A shy grin. "She was magical to me."

"She must have been quite something, then."

"I saw her photo and I *knew*. I had to find her."

"It was the same for me. Tell me about her, John.

"Oh you know all about her, Martha. *It* was *you*."

"Me? A home-wrecker! Oh God, I'm so sorry."

"I'm not. That photo led me right into my life."

My eyes filled as I looked up at him.

"Hey, Martha. Smile like you did in *the* picture."

"You're a trickster, John. And a very good man."

Together, we went to all-night movies and all-night diners. The movies were second rate; the food was better: homemade pies, fresh coffee, hot rolls. For me, such nights were companionable and comforting — salvation from my agonies alone on the studio floor. Still, I knew, John would not always be there for me. He was in and out of my studio already.

John danced on Broadway whenever he could. He had been in *Oklahoma!* and *On The Town.* He was dear, decent, devoted, but I still ached for my husband and my marriage. Abandonment was humiliating; it was only surpassed by a stark sense of aloneness, even as I resumed my teaching schedule. John could keep me from tears, but they were never far away.

Sensing this, when summer came, John took me on a holiday to Fire Island's beaches, just a ferry ride from Manhattan's steaming sidewalks. Late one afternoon, as we strolled on the boardwalk, a vicious storm blew up. The sky went black, thunder rumbled near, the wind blew hard and stiff. We walked faster, trying to reach shelter before the cloud-burst.

A sudden flash of lightning showed two missing boards directly ahead of me, forming a lethal shaft to the ground, far below. John jerked me back from the edge — just in time. I was grateful and regretful all at once. I told John I wished he'd let me fall. Worried, then, he frowned. He and others had feared my despair might turn suicidal, and he kept his eye on me.

What kept me going, in the end, was the persistent sense of my artistic calling. This was a gift from God; such gifts were never to be lost or tossed away. Eventually, bolstered by John's companionship and sympathy, my pain lessened, though it never left me completely. Even after our season of closeness, John always said I meant the world to him. While he did another stint on Broadway, I turned back to choreography. The result was my last solo ballet.

~~~

The Triumph of Joan of Arc premiered in 1951. It was an impressive piece about the great French heroine who felt destined to save her country. A peasant girl, guided by heavenly voices, she became an inspired military leader. Her mysticism fascinated me. How intriguing, I thought: an eighteen year old girl who could hear the voices of three saints. Surely such things could be. No saintly voices for me, but my own sense of vocation helped in the creation of this ballet.

Even so, the role was a demanding one for me, culminating in Joan's martyrdom. Captured by the enemy, abandoned by her friends, "The Maid" was burned at the stake in the marketplace in Rouen. I set myself to dance this agonizing death, while lights gave the effect of flames. Physically and emotionally draining, this ballet left me tired and disappointed in myself. I surveyed my work with a critic's eye.

Weak, I judged my own performance.

Lame. Restrained. Lacking focus.

I saw flaws, gaps, and an odd reticence in my usually intense choreography. I was also disappointed in myself for other reasons. I knew I was well beyond a dancer's usual retirement age: forty to forty-five or so. Somehow, I thought, I would prove to be an exception. At fifty, limber as a girl, I had danced the bride's role in *Appalachian Spring.* At fifty-six I had danced the demanding role of the evil queen, Medea. *Dance can punish those who love it*, I thought. And that thought enraged me.

Now I could no longer master movements I had always done with ease. My stamina had started to decrease. My extensions did not reach so high. My splits were not as wide. Worse, I had developed that affliction every dancer feared: arthritis. The disease was already twisting my hands. I hoped the arthritis would stop there. In all likelihood, though, it would advance. I would have to put less stress on my body.

I made my own private decision: I would not perform alone again, without my company's support. Even harder was giving up my starring roles to younger dancers. It was hard for me to watch them soar through choreography I had originated, lived and breathed and danced myself.

In most other professions, I would not be considered "old." But as a dancer I was no longer considered "young." I could not deny what my body told me. "Movement never lies," my father had repeated. I had to find a way to keep working within new limitations.

The most difficult ballet for me to surrender was my most popular work: *Appalachian Spring*. This would always be a deeply personal statement of love for me. It was all I had left of my romance and my marriage. Now others would dance the roles Erick and I had originated while we were still deeply in love.

When *Appalachian Spring* was revived and recast, I confessed my feelings to the company: This premiere would be one of the hardest days in my life. Some understood; some did not. One dancer was reduced to tears. Even so, I could not bear to watch a new couple dance my valentine to Erick.

~~~

He was having his own struggles, I knew, still trying to make a breakthrough at the age of forty-three. In 1952, he gave his independent debut in a solo performance at Hunter College in Manhattan. I dreaded this yet I felt compelled to attend. With John Butler and Bethsabee de Rothschild, I pulled my cloche hat over my eyes and entered the auditorium.

At the program's end, I sat motionless and saddened by what I had witnessed. No one wanted to discuss it. The three of us put away a bottle of wine at a café while we waited for the reviews. At last the papers came in.

Mr. Hawkins' performance lacked originality, the critics said — worse, it seemed reminiscent of Martha Graham. His dancing was "indifferent." How those reviews must have wounded and enraged him. Did he walk the streets alone, again? A string of failed concerts followed for Erick. I slipped into the back row at each and every one. The reviews were always poor. His breakthrough eluded him for years.

After reading Erick's disappointing press, I retreated to my dressing table. I thought of all the hopes he had shared with me, and I with him, only a few years before. A bout of "the glooms" threatened to creep into my bones. This time, Louis Horst was not there to sit by my bedside or lure me out by playing Scott Joplin's *Maple Leaf Rag* on the piano.

Nearing seventy, Louis had suffered a major heart attack. It was my turn to sit at *his* bedside and offer what comfort I could give. I saw how much he had changed over the years. His belly formed a mound under the sheet. His teeth had yellowed; his scalp showed through his thinning white hair. I remembered Louis as he had looked twenty years before; thirty years before. Now, in that spare hospital room, we reconciled as friends.

"Like your dress." Louis was still courtly.

"Homemade, as usual. You remember."

"Makes you look nineteen again."

"Louis, dear, I'm here to cheer *you* up."

"Done. Wasn't sure if you would come."

"I couldn't be anywhere else," I told him.

"Never knew if I really mattered to you..."

"Do you know now?" I bit my lip

"I do." A smile creased his face.

"Don't worry," I said. "You'll survive."

"Can you tell? You wouldn't humor me?"

"I *know*. You're playing piano on your covers."

"You noticed." Louis looked quite pleased.

"Of course. What's the musical selection?"

"*La Cabeza*. It's a tango. Can you do it?"

"*Can* I?" I tangoed solo from the room.

"Brava," Louis called.

In the hall, I wiped my eyes. Louis would recover, I believed, but his health would never rebound. His heart attack had been severe; the heart muscle itself was permanently damaged. I had to help support him now, as he had once helped to support me. I moved him into a new apartment in my neighborhood and watched him as he struggled to hold on.

I thought of Louis, a cigar clamped in his teeth, both feet planted under every theatre's backstage sign reading *NO SMOKING*. I thought of him looking up from his novel for my audition for Denishawn. It all seemed a long time go. My images of Louis seemed to dwindle and grow distant, as if he were retreating from me, passing over a hilltop and beyond my sight.

~~~

After I returned home from the hospital, I sat down at my safe place, my old dressing table. There I held myself quiet and still and concentrated on deep breathing. When I felt balanced once again, I did not look into the mirror. Instead I looked within, scanning my own personal landscape. Its changes were drastic and disturbing, with only haze ahead.

My divorce from Erick was final. Louis was slipping away. I remembered that day on Fire Island, when John Butler jerked me back from the board-walk's deadly gap. I studied a photo of myself on that trip, the day after John had rescued me from a fatal fall. It was he who had snapped this photo. In the picture I saw something of a spark in my gaze; the mouth, unsmiling, looked weary of living.

"You could let go," I told the picture in my hand.

"You don't want that," the photo seemed to say.

"You could simply fade away," I said aloud.

"Not that, either." The snapshot seemed to frown.

"What *do* you want, you aging dance-queen? "

"More life." The answer came. "More dance."

"What else?" I murmured to the photograph.

"You want to dance until you drop."

In 1954, the gifted dancer, Bertram Ross became my partner. With him, I led my company on a second tour of Europe — a triumphant one, this time. London, alone, remained reserved, but a new patron materialized there: Robin Howard, wealthy and cultured, raved. He was completely overwhelmed by the Graham troupe's opening performance.

Not only did Howard attend every show for two weeks straight, he invited me and the entire company to an Elizabethan banquet in his mansion. I was seated in "the Queen's chair." I made John Howard my "knight" and soon he took that part, to my surprise, in daily life.

Howard wanted my partnership in a new venture. He wanted us to become co-founders of first Graham School of Dance in England. *I can do this,* I told myself. *I don't need Erick to negotiate this.* With care and caution, I thought out Howard's proposal. In the end, my deal with him was this: If he would fund the school, I would offer free tuition. "Done," he said.

Thrilled by its winning streak, the company moved on to Copenhagen, Brussels, Germany and Switzerland. In the Swiss audience was the famed psychoanalyst, Carl Jung, who was also struck by the performance. He came backstage after the premiere to offer congratulation. We had an extraordinary "synergy,"and a long evening together. I found Carl attractive; looking back, I regret what might have been.

When the Martha Graham Dance Company returned from this triumphant tour, the routine of classes and rehearsals began with renewed vigor. I felt as if I had indeed begun to heal. I went on to rework *The Triumph of St. Joan* into a more imaginative dance, renamed *Seraphic Dialogues.* I was gratified by the result; the piece was far more than improved — it was salvaged. This time I avoided a solo work. Instead, I shared it with the company.

Since Joan of Arc believed she heard the voices of three saints, I cast three dancers to personify the Voices. Danced by Bertram Ross, Saint Michael, the Archangel, was brilliant. The concept for the revamped piece was lively and imaginative and this time I was satisfied with what I had done. *Rarely can you go back and correct the mistakes in your life*, I thought. *This time somehow it happened.*

~~~

It also happened that President Eisenhower's Administration had watched my company's European tour with interest and approval. In 1955, I was invited by the State Department to become my country's cultural ambassador abroad: the first American dancer to receive such an offer.

At sixty-one, I led my dancers on the first of many worldwide tours as cultural ambassadors. This was a far cry from those national bus tours, everyone agreed. Even so, from time to time, younger dancers suffered heatstroke, exhaustion, bouts of dysentery on long trips through East and West. As the oldest member of the company, I am proud to say I never missed a single performance.

In addition to the productions, I gave dance lectures and movement demonstrations whenever my troupe entered a new country.

"Reach, reach, reach."

"I never forget that," a dancer said.

"Curve your shoulders. Move from your core."

"Reach for the stars, with grounded feet."

"I remember," another dancer said.

Our international tours encompassed Western Europe, Scandinavia, the Near and Far East, Japan and China. The State Department briefed me before the first excursion began: At the height of the Cold War, my travels could strengthen ties with America's friends and allies. There was to be no propaganda, no patriotic speeches, no foreign services observers — in sight, at least. This time, international diplomacy came only through one universal language: the medium of modern dance.

As expected, the Soviet Union persisted in barring our troupe. The "sensuality" of my choreography was always the official explanation. The Kremlin did not find such "explicit" movement suitable for the Soviet people. I was amused and took this prohibition as a compliment. Romania was the only Iron Curtain country to accept the American dancers, but everywhere the troupe appeared, it was met with warmth, attentiveness and praise.

"Do you like it?" I asked.

"*Verdenderend,*" I heard in Holland.

"What do you think?" I queried.

"Magnifico," I heard the Italians say.

"Was it okay?" I asked again.

"Myougi," the Japanese enthused.

"How'd we do?" I repeated.

"Esplendidez," the Spanish told me.

"How was it?" I asked once more.

"Stor," the Danish people cheered.

My company's repertoire connected instantly with Korean and Japanese dancers. Our spare sets and stark movements had much in common with Asian dance principles. There were also echoes of Kabuki and Noh Theatre in my work. In Japan, an almost familial bond developed.

The same feeling extended to a trip through China. My emphasis on the breath's centrality was akin to the Chinese concept of space, central to martial arts and healing. Without realizing it, I had happened on techniques entirely new to the West, yet thousands of years old in the East.

In Japan, as well as other nations, audiences clamored for our own Graham Schools of Dance. Gradually, these schools were planted in almost every host country. I'm proud to say such terms as the "Graham Technique" and "Graham Contraction" became internationally recognized phrases.

I remembered talking with my father about my sense of inner power. That was long ago; at the time such power scared me. "Then use it for the good," my father had said. *"Build. Love. Bless."* Now, I hoped, I was living out his charge. I wished he could have watched us play to audiences of 2,000 in Tokyo and to crowds of 5,000 in Rangoon, Burma.

In some Eastern cultures, I learned, audiences cooked their dinners during a theatrical performance. At our Burmese shows, people arrived at outdoor theatres with pots, food, and small stoves. As I danced roles from Greek mythology and American experience, I caught the sharp-sweet scent of Indonesian curries. Somehow the different cultures blended together without any strain or effort.

Like the rest of the company, I shipped home special objects to remind me of each country I had visited. My great bed was sent all the way from Malaysia to New York. The bed would became my ultimate sanctuary — and my last large purchase, I suspected. Several new ideas would spring to mind in that sheltering space; even my insomnia seemed less irksome there. In this bed I hoped to think and read, find new stories and recast old ones. And in this bed, I hoped to die. Someday. Not yet.

This was not a reflective season in my life, however. I feared too much introspection. I made certain I was busy; so busy I could not grieve so hard for Erick. When I was not on tour, I had a demanding teaching schedule at my own studio and at the Juilliard. School of Music. Students were enthused and intrigued.

"Martha made you feel you could do anything," one said. Remarks like bolstered me when I needed that. Glenn Tetley, a principal Graham dancer, felt my classes restored his physical and spiritual balance. As Tetley struggled with an injured knee, I helped him to believe that he dance again. I refrained, however, from giving him my typewriter to lift with his leg.

~~~

My image as "nurturer" got little press.

My image as "temperamental tigress" did.

This was especially true after my most ambitious work, based on the character of a mythic Greek queen, drawn from the ancient trilogy by Aeschylus..

Clytemnestra was consigned to Hades to look back over her life and her sins. Was my attraction to this role a premonition? I could not have known that part of Clytemnestra's story would mesh with my own. I never knew how the idea occurred to me. Nor did I know I would play this role in life — and after life.

I designed the long production so I could remain on stage throughout three grueling acts. Nearing sixty-five, I was no longer able to dance for a sustained length of time. My arthritis had worsened, spreading through my body and almost crippling my hands now. Offstage I wore bell sleeves or elegant gloves to hide my twisted fingers.

But for this work on stage, I made a surprise decision. Instead of concealing my deformed hands, I used them to enhance the evil power of my character. I chose to expose a sight most people would disown; I knew this gesture served the larger work. I would sacrifice vanity for art — but at a cost I had not foreseen.

In *Clytemnestra's* opening sequence, I slithered toward the footlights. Abruptly I bared my gnarled hands, like talons now, as if to claw the air in front of me. Then I pointed my hands at the audience. There was always a gasp. The central character had made a memorable entrance, setting the tone for the story. While my company did most of the actual dancing, I concentrated on the acting in the piece.

Facial expressions and gestures became increasingly important. Finally, Clytemnestra had to review her death as well as her life. I would dance toward a dais, where I would lie with my head back, my face to the audience, as I waited for Orestes, danced by Bertram Ross, to "cut my throat" with a gleaming dagger.

During one performance, Ross, could not find the dagger anywhere onstage. Without informing us, the prop man had placed the weapon in a new hiding place. I was moving toward my death on the dais when Ross danced toward me, unplanned. For the next few moments, we communicated with gestures and whispers before a packed house.

"*No dagger,*" Ross whispered.

"Where?" I gestured with one hand.

"Anywhere," he hissed at me.

"Check the throne," I motioned.

"Aha! Here it is. Hidden well."

"I'll lie back. Do me in, dear."

"At your service, Madame."

Throughout these maneuvers, the baffled company looked on and tried to remain calm. The audience thought our interchange was part of the show. Still regal, I swept into position, lay back, bared my throat and was "dispatched" with the elusive dagger. This was hardly a comedic moment but afterwards, in the wings, Bertram and I could not contain our laughter. The prop man had disappeared. After several curtain calls, the company gathered to hear what prompted that "improv" around the throne.

Theatre-goers found *Clytemnestra's* dark plot mesmerizing, as audiences have for 2,500 years. The complex weave of scenery, costuming, dance and drama kept onlookers riveted throughout a long evening. The plot built suspense and the dancers were at peak performance.. The response to this production was laudatory. *The New York Times* led the press in calling *Clytemnestra* a masterpiece of ritualized drama.

The work was also a marriage of dance and theatre — a new form at that time. On tour again in 1958, at the age of seventy-four, I took this dance-drama to

Portugal. With my company, I performed *Clytemnestra* in Lisbon's enormous bull ring. The performance was sold out.

As it ended, the audience, some 2,000 strong, rose to its feet and cheered. I was overwhelmed as I stood in that ancient echoing arena. I could not speak, I could not move. And still the cheers went on: *Ole! Martha Graham, Ole!*

This was the culmination of my life's work. So I always told myself; so I always believed. I did not realize then how my role in this ballet revealed my age and fragility. After *Clytemnestra,* there was a new wariness when people spoke of me and, of course, I heard what was said.

In the press and in the studio and in the dance world at large, two questions began circulating, first in whispers, then in murmurs, then in gossip, then in print — and finally out loud. These were the persistent queries:

How long would I try to keep on dancing?

How long could I remain on stage?

∎

CHAPTER ELEVEN

The view from Hades can be harsh.

Even so, you cannot quit; you must watch it all. The hardest part is seeing yourself at your worst. Imagine this: you are jet-lagged, red-eyed, drenched, bedraggled, standing under harsh lights at a mirror in an airport where, through your own fault, you have missed the last flight out.

You squirm? So do I. Especially as I face this next section of the "scan." I have always called it my "dark passage." Before any images appear, I hear the sound of my own voice, on the phone, late at night.

"*Die while you're still beautiful.*"

A pause. And then I'd hang up.

Another of my late-night calls.

Who would mind my little messages?

Surely they were harmless enough.

What time was it? I kept losing track.

Where had I last seen my address book?

I was losing things more often, it seemed.

Ah. Here was the address book, on my desk.

Everything is perfectly all right, I whispered.

My apartment answered me with silence.

I am fine. I poured myself another drink.

The next morning I was not even sure I'd made those late-night calls. They had an air of hazy unreality about them; perhaps I'd thought them up but never made them. At the studio, there was never any comment. Surely everybody there was quite familiar with my voice. Maybe I had dreamed these small events. Sometimes, alone at midnight, I could not tell dreaming from reality.

Things were always better after a drink. The aloneness. And the arthritis. It did not respond to aspirin now. Other medications made me sick. No drugs. I would keep control over my own life. Hadn't I managed that so far? There was no reason to suppose I could not manage in the future. Was there? People seemed to watch me just a bit more closely now, I thought. Then again, I might be imagining that. Always sensitive, I felt I had to remain on the alert to run a company.

Certainly I refused to fret about my drinking. Alcohol muted an array of agonies. It kept me going, working, creating, and dancing. I could handle it. I always had. No one knew but Louis: for decades I had begun each day with one shot of Irish whiskey. No one smelled it and I quickly burned it off.

The drinking had worsened after Erick left, I knew. It had always been my secret, Of course, I never let alcohol interfere with my work. In fact, it enabled me to work. That was the main thing, of course, for me: to go on working.

Lately I needed just a bit more to drink after a workday. The arthritic pain was worsening; I almost hobbled now. *Getting old is a pain in the neck,* I once told the press. I had not wanted to use the word "ass." In fact, I had not wanted to make that statement at all. It wasn't true. *Getting old is hell, especially for dancers.* That was what I had wanted to say. If I had another chance, I would definitely get that point across.

I told this to Geordie, my sister, one evening, while we put away a bottle together. Geordie thought my comments were hilarious. Geordie, who also drank, laughed more often now with me. As sisters we might spend a few hours together, always at my flat, every two weeks or so. That was where Geordie stunned me with a new disclosure:

"Father had a fondness for the drink, you know."

"*What?*" I stared. "He couldn't have."

"Why not? Remember how calm he was?"

"I thought that was just...just Father's way."

"Remember his late-night rambles for sweets?"

"You mean—?" I sat stunned. "Whiskey?"

Geordie nodded. "It got worse after you left."

"I never smelled it. Only his pipe, his soap...."

"And cough drops. They really did the job."

"Oh my God." I gasped. "He was devious."

"Aren't we all?" Geordie shrugged.

Geordie laughed at my shock and then I was laughing at myself. This comradery was something of a comfort, since many of my older friends seemed somewhat different, even distant now. Hard to say exactly why. Certainly no one knew about the drinking. Like my father, I thought, I hid it well. And wasn't I just as productive as ever?

My ballet, *Acrobats of God*, had been a success. *Pheadre*, another venture into Greek mythology, had been deliciously controversial. The State Department found the work too "erotic" to be used on tour. *Pheadra* was even denounced by Congress. This had generated such a run on tickets, the show had completely sold out. Controversy over sex had always done wonders for show business. What a laugh I had with Geordie over that. We were able to enjoy each other at last. It had taken far too long for us to draw closer.

Poor Geordie. She looked frayed, graying, disheveled — once the beloved baby, the prettiest and sweetest of the three Graham girls. Auburn curls; she'd had masses of them. Creamy skin. Scores of beaux. Now a widow, working at the Graham school, Geordie drank during the day and this, at last, drew comment. I would not listen to a word of it. To the end, I protected and supported my youngest sister who seemed worn, weary, disappointed and — that awful word again — old.

Die while you're still beautiful, I thought again.

~~~

"Can we talk?" Bertram Ross looked at me.

"What's the matter?" I scanned his face. I'd known him a long time; he'd started classes with me after the war, on the GI Bill. He had grown into a dark, muscular dancer who was close to perfection, in my eyes. We were dance partners and friends; only that. But we could be honest with each other. I had a feeling we were heading into painful honesty just now.

"Darling, you don't *have* to dance anymore."

"I do. Of all people, you should understand that." I held his probing gaze. "I'm a dancer and that's all I've ever been. Take that away and there's nothing left. I'd lose my will to live if I stopped dancing."

We were sitting in my dressing room at the studio. Class was over for the day. Amber light splashed the walls and seemed to gild the dressing table mirror. The table itself was bright with flowers, photos, and framed awards. I sipped Earl Grey tea from a Wedge-wood cup. Its distinctive aroma filled the room. So did an uneasy pause.

"You're a genius choreographer," Ross said then.

"I am always a dancer first." I emphasized each word.

"Some of us are concerned about you, Martha"

"No need. I'm grand. We're in rehearsal with a new ballet. The company is strong and dancing at its best. We've had another European tour." I paused for effect. "I'll announce this soon. New funding is coming in from the Wallaces. You know they own *Reader's Digest,* don't you? I have to take credit for that connection. There's absolutely nothing to concern you, dear. Is there?" I raised my voice. "Or anyone else who's out there in the hall."

"Lila Wallace?" Ross was intrigued, of course.

"Not bad, hmm?" My voice took on an edge. "Do you know how we got the Wallace backing? Or would you rather see me as a useless menopausal harpy?"

"Martha! I don't think that. And you know it."

"I think half the company does, though."

"Not at all. No way. Absolutely not."

" 'Methinks thou dost protest too much.' "

"Oh Martha. Believe me, I'm not the enemy."

"Here's the story. Perhaps you might pass it on. Once there was a fine young man who grew terribly depressed." I took a sip of tea. "Ben was on the point of taking his own life. Friends took him to see one of our ballets — *Errand Into the Maze.* You remember?"

"Of course. Your third Greek piece."

"Well, that work made Ben understand his darkness and get past it. He told me the piece restored his will to live. Ben just happens to be a close friend of Bill Kennedy, curator of the Wallace art collection. And Ben swore he would do anything he could to help us. Well, he has. He won us serious attention from the Wallaces. It all started with my dance. Do you think I'm failing the company, Bert?"

"It's just...well, no," Ross said. "It's not that."

"It's my dancing. Isn't it? You all want me to stop. Oh yes, I hear things. You're not the only one who thinks I'm too old to keep going." I raised my voice again. "In case your comrades are listening...let me tell you this, my dear. I'll announce it soon. I'm going on tour in Israel with *Judith*. It opens at the Habima Theatre in Tel Aviv this fall."

I watched Ross absorb this before I went on. "An Israeli composer did new music. Bethsabee de Rothschild is thrilled. She's bringing her Bat Dor Dance Company to the premiere. Remember how so many in her troupe trained here? And some of our dancers have joined Bat Dor, of course. It will be quite a reunion."

"Really." Ross looked at me. "Another *coup*."

"Bethsabee's so generous with us. But Bertram..."

"No more surprises. I've had enough for today."

"Didn't you want to raise some pressing concern?"

Bertram Ross looked down. "I don't think so."

"Excellent." I smiled. "Anything else?"

"Not...at the moment." Ross sighed. "You witch."

"Careful. That makes you a warlock, Bertram."

"That's all right. Sorcery has its place."

"Once I make my announcements, we'll have no need of sorcery. The Wallace lawyer will be setting up a new foundation for us. A trust fund for life." I raised my voice. "His name's McHenry. In case anyone out there wants to know. He'd like to chair our board of directors." I smiled again. "Enjoy your evening — all of you."

Ross had to laugh as he left the room. We could both see figures standing in the hall. Shameless eavesdropping, I called it. This was rampant in every dance company or theatre group, of course, but I liked to stay on top of it. For the moment, I knew that mission was accomplished.

The witch had won a stay of execution.

Of course, I knew, it would not last for long.

"The battle's just beginning," I said aloud.

~~~

Two heroes contended on the stage.

Their striped shields whirled like chariot wheels.

This time, I presented another interpretation of a Greek myth. The ballet, *A Cortege of Eagles,* featured a survivor of the Trojan War: Hecuba, that great matriarch, mourning her family, all lost through warfare's horrors. The dance-drama widened the scope of grief I had shown in my early ballet, *Lamentation.* Now that grief encompassed the entire fallen world.

Hecuba, as I envisioned her, was in anguish over the uselessness of combat in all eras and all cultures.

I know this woman, I thought as I read of Hecuba in my books of Greek mythology. *I know this grief.* I had lived through two world wars, the Korean War, and now another kind of combat: The human struggle with mortality itself. At my age, I could look back on a long series of losses in my life. I lamented all of them as I danced Hecuba's role in *Cortege of Eagles.* Late at night, I grieved alone, never wanting to depress my fragile sister, Geordie. I seemed to be outliving almost everyone I cared about.

During technical rehearsals for *Cortege,* my longtime lighting designer, ill with cancer, was released from the hospital to work on one more Graham production. Jean Rosenthal and I had been close friends for decades and we both knew *Cortege* would be our final effort together. This was left unspoken — until Jean collapsed in the midst of work.

She was rushed back to the hospital. Shortly after she was settled there again, her long struggle with cancer ended. When Jean's personal assistant appeared at a rehearsal for *Cortege,* I saw the news on the assistant's face. Jean was dead. At peace, I tried to remind myself. That night on stage I grieved within my role — but also on a personal level. I dedicated my performance to Jean Rosenthal.

At home, alone, after the dance-drama's successful premiere, I poured myself a whiskey and looked over my photographs. Before I could move past my father's image, I had drained my glass, only to refill it. The dramatic persona of Hecuba was leading me into a review of all my losses. It had seemed the perfect role, but its timing was destructive. Every time I went onstage as the grieving matriarch, I relived each period of mourning in my life.

I could not look at Erick's photographs — and there were many. I could hardly bear to glance at the many snapshots of me with Louis; he had died shortly after I gave him a party to celebrate his eightieth birthday. He'd always said he was the string to my kite. He gave me discipline; he'd kept me connected to the ground. Now that kite seemed lost in an immense and empty sky.

Gone, too, were dancers from my company who had moved on to new endeavors: Merce Cunningham, John Butler, Glenn Tetley, Pearl Lang and Sophie Maslow among them. A few left with bitterness about my tight control of the studio. Others had simply gone out on their own. It was natural, I knew, for them to grow up as artists. Still, these dancers were uniquely gifted and original. They could be replaced but never reproduced.

Each loss hurt, whether it was professional or personal. Hard times, I told myself, demanded toughness. I tried to maintain a sense of dignity and fortitude, even as I grieved. If I could survive Erick's departure, I must be able to survive new ones. And I could keep some grief to myself. When we lost our mother and our sister, Geordie and I sat together in the flat on 63rd Street and mourned privately, toasting memories with whiskey.

The subject of alcohol rose again in another place. Someone at the Graham studio took it upon himself to call Mary Wickes, my longtime therapist, to inform her of my drinking. At first Mrs. Wickes was angered by my deception; still, the therapist knew all about alcoholics in denial. Gray-haired, keen-eyed, and wise, Mrs. Wickes tried to probe the depths of my fears and pain.

"You're not immortal." Mrs. Wickes spoke gently.

"I'm not afraid of death at all," I snapped.

"Then what fears prompts the drinking?"

"Getting old. Ugly. Infirm. Too decrepit to dance."

"Did you hope to escape the human condition?"

"I did," I admitted. "I've lasted so long, you see."

"No dancer lasts that long. No dancer expects to."

"I've never been like other dancers," I said.

"You've danced into your seventies."

"My only instrument is *my own body*."

A dancer's body was like a musician's flute, a painter's brush, I tried to explain. I told *The Washington Post's* dance critic, Alan Kreigsman, how dancers' bodies are much like prized animals. We trained them, nourished, discipline and exercise them until they become an extension of our inner beings. I avoided descriptions of my own rage about the body's aging. It was never wise to give too much to the press, I knew. I did not want look as bitter as I felt.

And so I choked back feelings I dared not express. It was hard to deny my sorrow over the limits of my gift; my physical inventiveness, my power to turn emotion into movement you could see. I did not want to sound maudlin or pitiful. To stifle rage and pain, physical and emotional, to stave off the end of my career, I drank more, during the day, as well as late at night.

Sometimes when I came late to class or a rehearsal now, my dancers noticed an aura of alcohol around me. I heard them talking. Were my eyes really glazed? I did not see that in my mirror. I did not see so many things, just then. Never strong on patience, now I seemed to have none at all. Always hard on myself, I grew just as hard on others, leaving more than one dancer in tears.

My famous temper had mellowed while I was with Erick. Since he left and my drinking increased, I blew up more easily — and often unexpectedly. I remembered my dance-ballet, *Embattled Garden*, set in Eden itself. I had written a starring role for "Eve," played by one of my principle dancers, and one for "The Serpent," played by a principle male dancer. Looking back, I saw myself fly out of control at a rehearsal for *Embattled Garden*.

As "The Serpent," the male dancer perched in an artfully constructed "tree," designed by that patient sculptor, Osamu Noguchi. The ballet opened when "The Serpent" leapt down from the tree and made intense advances on "Eve." I stood silent, making mental notes as the rehearsal began. Suddenly I sprang from observation to outrage. My voice rose to a shout; I called a halt to the action. This was all wrong, I knew. Lashing out, I pushed "Eve" aside and took her place.

This time, when "The Serpent" came down from the tree, I was waiting. Still strong, I took control, lunging forward and pressing myself against the male dancer, groin to groin, forcing him backward with my body. There was something of *Xochitl* about my fierce movements — so fierce, my combs scattered to the floor and my hair burst from the chignon at the nape of my neck.

When my demonstration of the scene has over, I turned on the shaken dancers. *That*, I said, was what I wanted. Passion. Conflict. Intensity. The crucial concept in *Embattled Garden* was, indeed, a battle. I would not have my work watered down. Nor was it. When the piece was finally presented, it won rave reviews. *But at what cost*, I wondered afterwards. Two more dancers soon defected from the Graham company.

There were other situations that shamed me — too late, too late, I knew. I had failed two good friends badly. Robin Howard, my gallant English patron, had sold real estate to raise funds for me. Everyone knew of his generosity. At the end of a successful London season, when I took my curtain call, I omitted thanks to Howard and gave the evening's tribute to my dress designer Halston. Robin Howard could not control his tears.

Worse still, I had failed Louis Horst. At seventy-nine, he had been invited to receive his first and only honorary doctorate from Wayne State University in Detroit, Michigan. This had been arranged by the chair of Bennington's dance program and another former colleague. I was also slated to receive a degree at the same ceremony.

The main focus, however, was on Louis Horst. This honor meant more to him than he could express; academic recognition would finally outweigh his lack of higher education. But how would he get to Detroit? Ill and aging, he could no longer travel alone. To his immense relief, I would accompany him on the grueling journey; this, he sensed, might be his last. Louis had been looking forward to this honor for several months; it would put the culminating shine on his career.

On the appointed day, at the appointed hour, Louis stood alone in Grand Central Station. I was not there. Looking back now, I shudder at the image of his solitary figure: His white head bent, his shoulders stooped, his blue eyes hopeful, then frantic, then concerned. Finally, he phoned a mutual friend to check on me. When I was contacted at home, I was disheveled, not packed and not dressed to go anywhere at all. I heard the fury and disgust in our mutual friend's voice. Horrified, I glanced at my watch.

How could I have forgotten my appointment with Louis? In haste, I prepared to meet him, but by the time I reached the station, the right train was long gone. After hours of waiting on a bench, Louis looked tired and defeated. He placed a nitroglycerin tablet underneath his tongue; I rattled out profuse apologies.

"Oh darling, I'm so very sorry, but we'll get there."

"In time?" He sighed. "We might."

"We'll make it. I know this means so much to you."

"What the hell do you care? You weren't coming."

"I was. I was just delayed. I said how sorry I am."

"Selfish. You always were. You never change."

I flinched. "How can you talk to me that way?"

"You don't give a damn about anybody else."

"Of course I do. I came, I'm here, we're going soon."

"You're so self-centered you see nothing."

"My Luigi. I see *you*." I touched his hand.

"Don't pretend. You don't give a crap about me."

"You want to go alone?" I said stiffly.

"You know I can't. And I'm too beat to argue."

The next train ride, early in the morning, exhausted Louis further. The car arranged to meet us wasn't waiting. Finally, we reached Wayne State's assembly hall — just as the awards ceremony ended. Louis received his long-awaited doctorate in near-silence. The audience was absent, the applause was nil, as was any fanfare.

Louis read his carefully composed acceptance speech to an empty hall. Wayne States' dean read out his own speech, lauding Louis's contributions to music and dance. Two professors stayed and clapped politely.

The weak patter of applause sounded flat in the large auditorium. And then there was the long train trip home. When we got back to New York City, Louis was worn out, unsteady, and wracked with angina.

Furious with myself, I tried to make up for my part in this fiasco. At my studio, I arranged an expensive party for Louis on his eightieth birthday, just a few weeks later. Everyone he cared for was invited and there were flowers, decorations, and a throne for the guest of honor.

Behind the throne, Bertram Ross had created an original backdrop: Floor-to-ceiling strings of multi-colored gumdrops. Loving statements were read aloud and champagne toasts were offered. Louis looked appreciative but ashen and worn out. Looking on, I wondered if this tribute was an honor — or an ordeal for him. I felt a sudden chill at the back of my neck.

One week after the party, Louis fell in the lobby of his apartment building — another heart attack; another wailing ambulance. Another hospitalization. Four days later, Louis Horst was dead. I stood with his young girlfriend at his bedside.

The editor of the obituary page called me from *The New York Times.* I offered a lengthy statement praising Louis for all he gave to modern dance and, of course, to me. *Too little, too late,* I thought, afterwards. *Perhaps too much, too late.*

That night I invited my sister, Geordie, to share a drink at my flat on 63rd Street. We settled into the comfortable living room, and I, still weeping, poured the drinks. On the third round, Geordie suddenly grew brave. Her hazel eyes, usually wide and docile, narrowed at me.

"How could you give that party for Louis?"

I refilled our glasses and turned. "What? Why?"

"You knew he wasn't up to it." My sister fixed me with a look. "That was the last thing he needed."

"I was trying to make up for that awful trip."

"The party wasn't for Louis, it was for you."

"Geordie." I stared. "You don't really mean that."

"That was your way of absolving yourself."

"I wanted Louis to feel happy, loved."

Geordie stood unsteadily. "No. *You* did."

"I didn't know you could be cruel Geordie."

"It's always about you, Martha, isn't it?"

I stood to face my sister. This frightened child-woman, this mousy, timid, muddled baby sister had summoned up a lifetime of resentments. It appeared, and hurled them all at me.

"Listen, Geordie." I looked at her. "I pay your rent, I give you taxi money, grocery money, a clothing allowance. I gave you a job at my school. And you have the gall to talk to me this way? How dare you?"

"It only took me sixty years or so." Geordie's laugh was bitter. "I was always terrified of you, Martha. You were so intense, so explosive. You ruled us girls. And then you were 'My sister, the star.' " Her laughter turned bitter. "Finally, I see what you really are. Why fear you now? You're just another selfish drunk. Like me."

Geordie grabbed her coat, lurched to the door, and slammed out.

~~~

Once again, I turned back to the only thing that transcended every misery: Dance. More friends urged me to retire or teach full-time. To every plea, I listened without saying a word. Then I would turn on my heel and leave the room. I believed my silence was more powerful than anything I could say in my own defense.

When I was angry, it was obvious. One of my dancers compared my rage to sheets of lightning contained in one room. My glances were electric, I was told. Never more so than now. As I walked through the studio, I'd pinch students who didn't stand up straight enough; I'd snarl at others.

I would not give up, even as dancing grew more dangerous for me — and everybody else on stage. I came later to rehearsals now, confident that my mind, my will, and muscles' memory would still get me through a show. My body was so well-trained it moved within its limitations. I thought it always would.

Meanwhile, I ignored a series of ominous signs. Harvard College invited me to a public ceremony in Cambridge, Massachusetts. There, at that prestigious institute of learning, I would be awarded an honorary doctoral degree. With an escort from the Graham company, I arrived safely in Cambridge; there I was warmly received.

In an academic gown and hood, I joined the processional of faculty and honorees toward the chapel. It was hard for me to keep my place in line. I felt as of the path's passing was uneven. I thought perhaps it was my shoes. I knew I was weaving as I walked; at one point, I nearly fell. No one was rude enough to ask me why.

Back in New York City, at Philharmonic Hall, a packed auditorium awaited me for a lecture. I rose and slowly approached the podium — without my notes. After a burst of welcoming applause, I began to speak. Was that my voice? I lost the drift of sentences I could not finish; I rambled off the point. My talk was a disjointed jumble. Again, no one was rude. Later, when I realized what I'd done, I blamed the failure on my missing notes.

Oblivious to danger, I plowed on. Surely, I thought, I could do a run of revivals, featuring my three-act ballet, *Clytemnestra.* I had limited the Greek queen's role, adjusting its movements to accommodate my arthritic limbs. I could do it; I *would* do it. I did. All went smoothly until one of my spiral falls. I'd done them for forty years; they were still within my range. Always before, I could spiral upwards once again to kneel and, at last, to stand. This time was different. Even as I spiraled downward, I knew it would happen.

I could not rise from the stage floor.

It seemed as if I lay there for several minutes. I could not make my body do as I willed; I went hot with fury and humiliation. Time stopped for me. I felt as if I floundered on the stage for an eternity. In fact, Bertram Ross moved so fast, I was only down for seconds. With one deft dip, he lifted me, improvised a turn, and set me down on a projection from the set.

Thanks to Ross, the audience never realized what happened. The rescue was so quick, the other dancers were not thrown off-cue and the ballet continued in time to the music. But cast and crew had seen it all, I knew. We had watched my faltering onstage, in need of rescue — for the first time in my life.

As usual, numerous curtain calls finished off the evening. With wounded dignity, I thanked Bertram Ross; then I retreated, as usual, to my dressing room. There I sat, shaking, before my mirror. Over and over again, I saw that helpless moment on the stage. In the glass, I saw an old woman's face, devastated and demonic. My hands trembled. I had *become* Clytemnestra — after the curtain was down.

This light is much too harsh, I told myself. *My reflection must simply be distorted by the glare.* I switched off the dressing table's lamps with a snap. The face before me did not change. *It's just the makeup,* I thought. *It's meant to exaggerate, I put it on myself.* Quickly, I wiped off the greasepaint, the blackened brows and eyeliner.

I was rinsing my face when a friend and colleague paid a call. The friend was Nathan Kroll, who had made a well-received film about me and my work: *A Dancer's Life.* Short, balding, kindly and intense, Kroll had always been adoring. Now, he said, he came on a mission: To urge his idol to slow down. The part of Clytemnestra was too demanding for me now.

"Martha, darling," Kroll pleaded. "Take a break."

"No one can do *Clytemnestra* with my soul."

"Just a break. From the show. From dancing."

I said nothing but I glared into his eyes.

"Please," he said. "Martha, I'm begging you."

"Without dance, I'm dead, and you know it."

"Rest, restore yourself. You don't have to die."

"Dance is my life, Nathan. My only way to live."

"You can teach, choreograph—"

"*I. Am. A. Dancer. First,*" I said distinctly.

"There's a time for every dancer to stand aside."

"Not for me, Nathan. I can't. That's all I can say."

Kroll's shoulders sagged. He kissed my hand.

"Goodbye, dear Martha." Nathan turned and left.

■

CHAPTER TWELVE

Was it time for a graceful exit from the stage?

This seemed to be everyone's desire except mine. I still felt I had more to give. Was this *hubris* — pride — or perseverance? The dilemma tortured me, waking and sleeping. No clear answer came to but one: I was a dancer. That was all I'd ever been. Without that, I was nobody. Life, for me, was dance. Take that away and I would lose my will to go on.

Even so, after my mishap on stage, every performance seemed to be a risk, a gamble, a waiting game. From then on, there was no use trying to conceal the sense of some inevitable disaster. No one knew how it would happen but it was building, nonetheless.

In order to go on dancing, I needed to go on drinking. It controlled my pain and gave me the confidence to keep working. I was not the first artist, or the last, to use alcohol as a support through the creative process. Sound defensive? I guess I was.

As I began notes for a new ballet, I drove myself forward. I tried to concentrate on work while gossip swirled about me. I was kept well informed. There was talk about my drinking, my arthritis, and my age. My business manager feared I would damage Graham's reputation; others shared his opinion. Finally, an old friend was summoned to intervene.

His mission was simple: Convince me to make a dignified departure from performing. Literally, with hat in hand, he paid a visit to my home. A gentleman and a respected actor, he had a distinguished and authoritative air about him. His pocket handkerchief was always crisply folded; his muted tie was drawn into a perfect knot. The man looked the part of a stern college professor.

No one made him nervous — until he visited me at my apartment. My presence somehow overwhelmed him, even as I offered him a chair, a demitasse, and cigarettes. I knew exactly why he was calling on me on that day. Someone from the studio had sent him on this uncomfortable errand. He cut through the niceties to the point he'd come to make.

"It's time to let go," he told me. "Let go of dancing."

"I will not." I was blunt. "Who sent you here?"

"There is a great deal of concern about you."

"Concern, concern. I don't believe that's it."

"Why keep on? No other dancer has."

"I've never been like other dancers. Have I?"

"Not the point. Let the company live and thrive."

"I've done that every day of my entire life."

My friend sighed. "You really have no choice."

"I always have a choice." My voice went cold.

"Your body will decide the issue. It won't obey."

"I think I know my own body better than you do."

He leaned forward. *"Your body can't go on."*

I sat silently, giving him my lightning glare.

"Friends care," he said. "Enemies await."

Without a word, I saw my guest to the door.

~~~

As I had been warned, the "enemies" were quick to act. An unnamed dancer slipped backstage after a performance of *Clytemnestra* and opened the door to my dressing room. Still in costume and makeup, I had just finished my curtain calls at City Center's theatre in Manhattan. It was midway through our 1967 season. The stranger, young and blonde, was a respected figure in dance circles, but I pretended not to recognize her.

"Who are you?" I demanded. "Why are you here?"

"You know me. I'm a soloist. You know where."

"I'll call the house manager." I stood by the door.

"Listen. You can't do this anymore."

"Who let you in?" I stared. "How dare you?"

"Exit gracefully. No humiliation."

"Get out," I shouted. "Get out right now."

"I'm offering to take over for you. Let me help."

I slammed the door in the intruder's face.

The next blows came from two important critics, one from *Dance Magazine*; the other, now the new and powerful dance critic of *The New York Times*. The first was gentler. My performances seemed "uncertain" now. Barnes was not gentle in the least. He referred to my current abilities in slighting terms and was not the least ambiguous about his message. Barnes ordered me to quit right now.

Upset, wounded, and outraged, I tried to refute him at the Brooklyn Academy of Music. There I was awarded the city's greatest honor for an artist: The Handel Medallion. As I accepted it, I delivered a brief speech — but this time, I could hear my own voice rambling. I lashed out at Clive Barnes. I vowed to go on dancing. *I* would decide when to stop; no one else would decide that for me.

News of this outburst reverberated throughout my school, staff, and company. I did not feel welcome in my own studio. In a temporary way, I solved the problem for everyone: I withdrew to my apartment like a wounded animal and rarely came out. Bertram Ross, one of Graham's artistic directors, worked with longtime principle Mary Hinkson. Together they managed to maintain the company and its dance school.

There was a mutinous mood among the dancers themselves. Some did not want me to return; I thought they feared I might bring them all down with me. The only one I trusted at that point was Tom. I did not know what to tell my company; I did not know what action to take. As 1968 unfolded, the dilemma was removed from of my hands.

Reader's Digest's Lila Wallace intervened. As Graham's major funder and board member, she had leverage, as well. Mrs. Wallace issued an ultimatum through her attorney, Barnabus McHenry. The message was unequivocal.. The Wallaces would cut all funding for my company if I did not stop dancing. I had to acquiesce — or lose the creation of my lifetime.

I chose to save my company. And with that company, I danced my last performance in my new ballet, *A Time of Snow*. At the end of the production, two aged characters lie dead on the stage: Heloise and Abelard. Danced by Bertram Ross and me, the figures presented a sharp contrast. Photos show me looking gaunt and almost spectral, while Ross, despite his makeup, was still young, strong, and vibrant.

The curtain came down on *A Time of Snow* on May 25, 1968. Later, I could not recall much about that final appearance. I had numbed myself and steeled myself too well. A quiet exit was all I wanted. No words. No tears. No farewells. In my dressing room, I dropped my brush and comb in a bag, along with my photos and makeup. Then, alone, I slipped out of the theatre through a back door on the alley. I still don't know how I got home.

~~~

My collapse came quickly.

Predictable — but predicted to be temporary.

Everyone remembered how well I had rebounded after Erick's desertion. Within a few weeks I was lifting weights and working on my own restoration program. Surely it would be the same way now. My sudden hospital stay was mere theatrics, cynics said. Others thought I'd had a nervous breakdown. Surely it would pass with rest.

Why, then, was I having so much difficulty breathing? Why did my lab work worry my doctors? *I will lose my will to live*, I'd said, *if I stop dancing.* But surely I was not powerful enough to bring on my own death. Was I? My hospital stay dragged on for months. I was in decline. Members of the company made calls. On oxygen, I could say little. My face looked ravaged. I'd let my hair go white. Agnes de Mille, was urged to visit right away. I was not expected to survive much longer.

In and out of consciousness, I saw blurred faces hanging above me. Fragments of words. *Better soon. Jaundice. Get well. Complications. Pressure low. Four liters. Lovely roses. Pulse erratic.* Words like that. My mind wandered back and forth in time. Images appeared but in no logical sequence:

At ten, I was running through a frozen field. At sixteen, I was entranced by a goddess. At twenty-eight, I was buying Louis sunflowers. At forty-six, I was lying in Erick's arms. At twenty-three, I was dancing with Madame in the long room. At fifty-six, I was alone in London. At twenty, I was standing at my father's grave. At twenty-three, I was dancing Xochitl at Denishawn....

For a long time, everything seemed to smear like a child's finger painting. Then, through a fog, I saw a face. Blue eyes. Spectacles. A long nose, a prim mouth. At the neck, a stethoscope. The face spoke.

"Miss Graham? Understand me?"

"Yes, Doctor. I understand you."

"You know where you are?"

"Hospital. New York City. 1968."

"Miss Graham, I must tell you..."

"Bad news. I see it in your eyes."

"You have diverticulitis, but it's minor."

"Will you tell the press, Doctor?"

"That part. Not the rest, it's private."

"Cancer? Like my sister, Mary?"

"Not cancer. Miss Graham...."

"Just tell me what I have. Please."

There was a long, tense pause.

"For God's sake, Doctor, what?"

"Cirrhosis of the liver. I'm sorry."

Another pause. "Will it kill me?"

"If you ever drink again, it will."

I looked up. "And if I don't?"

"Guarded optimism, as of now."

"I see." I lay there, stunned.

"Miss Graham, it's all up to you."

"I see that, too. I see too much."

"We're not out of the woods yet...."

Gradually the hospital room came into focus. It was private, light, and allowed me to see the river. Which river, I wondered? The East River or the Hudson? I must ask someone. There was a private nurse on duty — who called her in? And this airy pleasant room, filled with flowers. How had that been arranged? I suspected Bethsabee had telephoned instructions all the way from Tel Aviv, where she had moved to run her Batseva dance troupe. When was that? Five years, ten years ago? Ten. Definitely. 1958.

But Bethsabee could not be here by my beside. Visitors from the company slacked off. A young man on Graham's staff did come every day. I asked who sent him. No one had, he said. This was his own choice. He'd been at the studio a couple of years; his training was in business and journalism. He was helping out with the management end of things. What was his name? Tom, I thought.

That was not quite right but that's what I always called him. It became a private joke between us. He sat quietly with me. A good looking young man, fresh-faced, eager, clear-eyed and concerned. He stayed by my side throughout my long ordeal.

When a friend noted my white hair, I winced. She thought it was suitable for me to look my age. *I'll be damned if I do,* I thought. As soon as the friend left, I called my longtime hairdresser to the hospital. Soon I was a brunette again. Tom approved. He thought it was a good sign — a renewed interest in living.

But the next day, there was a setback. The fumes from the hair color must have affected my lungs, still sensitive. When I rose from bed to get to the bathroom, I could not breathe. The nurse was on break, the oxygen was across the room. I could not walk with any steadiness.

I wavered on my feet; I heard my breathing rasp — and then nothing more. When I opened my eyes again, I was looking into Tom's worried face. He was cradling my head with one arm. With the other hand, he was holding an oxygen mask over my nose and mouth. "Don't talk," he said. "Breathe. You'll be all right. Close call."

I saw yellow tulips scattered on the floor and Tom's briefcase, fallen open when he'd dropped it. He had come in just as I was passing out. Catching me before I could fall, he'd lain me on the bed and grabbed the oxygen tank, holding the mask over my face. Now I stared at him.

"You saved my life," I said quietly.

He held a finger to his lips and I stopped talking then. Angels come in disguise, Lizzie always said. *Even to me,* I thought. *With all my failings, all my terrible mistakes.* I was ashamed when tears ran down my face. *I must be meant to live.* The tears would not stop. How stupid, how selfish I had been. It was hard to look at myself now, without the haze of whiskey.

I quit drinking cold-turkey.

I have not touched alcohol again.

I willed myself to get through the shakes, the vomiting, the times of temptation. Friends offered me their Connecticut estate for a period of recovery. How tempting was its well-stocked bar. I called on the strength that helped me to rebuild my knee, so many years before. I locked the liquor cabinet and gave the key to Tom, my assistant now.

Finally, I started to grow stronger. I breathed in clean air, ate more, slept well. And finally, it was not quite so hard to resist a drink. The habit of a lifetime was broken, I felt, and I had done it on my own. In a way, I was just as proud of that as any of my ballets.

At last, I felt something like a fresh March wind blowing through me. I had not dared to hope I might feel that again. With Tom Smith I took long walks and sat by the fire. There we talked about serious and silly things. Dance and demons. Grilled cheese and tomato soup. A shared aversion to red licorice. Anecdotes from dance classes and business classes. His experience at journalism school. My experience at Denishawn. Tom said he had worked with a great diva of the stage. That turned our talk to theatre and to many things that did and did not have to do with the performing arts.

When I was ready, Tom would help me settle back into my flat. It would be soon. And soon, I felt ready to take charge of my company again. I would return to teaching and to choreography. I already had a plan for a new ballet — for my company, not for myself. Ideas still rose up in my mind, and images, and movements, and stories.

Without the whiskey, I used to fear my creativity would leave me. Now, to my amazement, it was stirring deep within me once again. At the end of my recovery period, I had been stone cold sober for one year, three weeks, and eleven hours. Some days it was hard. Most days it was good.

No more drinking — and no more dancing. I would miss dancing every day, but my company came first. I could still teach and choreograph ballets. Finally, I could accept this. Why? I wondered. Perhaps it was that moment when I locked eyes with Death — just as I once locked eyes with a lion. I had left the peril of that gaze and come away with a surprising gift: Another chance. After claiming that, I reached a new conclusion.

Once a dancer, always a dancer.

That identity could not be taken from me.

Dance is who I am. And it still was.

The day of my return home, I walked around my flat. My furniture, my photos' frames, my rugs and runners — all had a strange shine to them. My stage costumes had been hung up in the closets. My performance *Playbills* and my clippings had been laid out on the dining table. My silver handled brush and comb had been set out on my dresser. Yellow tulips seemed to bloom from every vase. I opened the drapes to let in more light.

Then I paused at the window — I had forgotten one last thing until that moment. In the kitchen, in a secret hiding place, there was an unopened bottle of whiskey. I had stashed it there two years before. Now, I reached up and took the bottle down. I weighed it in my hands. I opened it with care. That familiar scent rose toward me. I called Tom in to witness what I did. Then, with a steady hand, I poured the amber liquid down the kitchen sink.

As I watched the drain clear, I recalled the words I had spoken to myself two decades earlier. Then, abandoned by Erick, I had stood alone in a London hotel room, summoning a message to help me carry on. Now, I wanted to affirm those words once more. Some ritual should mark my return to life.

Indians believe there is an instant when a ritual chant changes from words to magic. I understood the truth of that belief. I had seen movement turn to magic throughout my decades in dance. Right here, in this kitchen, I wanted to repeat one talismanic phrase. It was more than words. It was an invocation. A promise. A credo.

"Where a dancer stands, that is holy ground."

"This must be the place." Tom set down my bags

~~~

If only the story could have ended there.

In a way, the worst was yet to come.

It was called "reorganization."

It was called "cleaning house."

It was called "a massacre."

When I returned to my school and company, I sensed a different atmosphere in what had once been my domain. The change was subtle but significant to me. My welcome was muted, I thought. My staff seemed somewhat distant. My company appeared wary of my presence. During my "dark passage," as I called it, mutual trust had broken down. Such a breakdown never could be mended, I knew.

This troupe would always wonder if I could stay sober. The possibility of relapse was not out of the question for them, as it was for me. The dancers and the staff could not know if they dared to count on me again. In turn, I did not dare to count on them. My business manager had turned against me, I was told, and had influenced others. I did not know how many, but the business manager quit when I returned.

To fill his place, I appointed Tom Smith. He was not a dancer but had business acumen. And he would never try to force me out. I felt he was one of the few people I could trust. For me, loyalty trumped artistic expertise as I struggled to survive this new challenge.

The company response to Tom's appointment was swift. Many of my dancers quit; they objected to an outsider who wasn't a dancer. Some, like Bertram

Ross, left on a gracious note. Others departed in anger or total silence. Part of the staff followed and some were let go. After moving on, many remained critical of me. A few of the "old-timers" stayed in place, hiding their mixed feelings.

The upheaval at Graham was the stuff of gossip, speculation, and hot news. I must take drastic action if my company and school were to endure, transcend the turmoil, and restore its reputation. I would start again with new dancers and a revamped staff. Throughout this crisis, I tried to keep a cool head, a keen eye, and a sound daily routine.

*I must see this through. I must...I must...*became my constant inner chant. And Tom Smith was my constant support. "New blood," he was called. It didn't matter to me that he had never been a dancer. What I needed now was a steady hand in business matters and a sense of trust. In him, I had both — and he would set the tone for others yet to come.

At the time, I felt I had acted on behalf of my company and my school. In fact, this seemed the only way to handle such a precarious situation. It was later that the doubts and the regrets began. I find it painful to look back on this period, even now. I wonder if I did the right thing and acted on the best advice. I grieved the loss of dancers I'd known so well for years. But I continued on. There was nothing else to do.

By 1974, there was a new stability to my establishment. Tom had played a crucial role in this effort and he remained attentive to my every need. I had been conducting dance classes again, almost every day;

I lectured widely — and lucidly — throughout New York. Tom's blonde head could be seen wherever I was: at those lectures, in the studio, and at glittering awards ceremonies. There were thirty years between us but I never felt them. Nor did he, I believed. Every year, Tom marked my birthdays with personal gifts: costly jade, coral, and turquoise jewelry; sculpted glass, original artwork. These were presented with champagne and roses at the best tables in Manhattan's best restaurants.

Tom understood when I mourned the loss of my dancing. He seemed to sense the empty place that left in my life. Once he found me weeping in the studio, early one morning. I explained what I was missing, wiped my eyes, squared my shoulders, and went out to teach another class.

Now, I turned to new ventures into choreography. Following my studio's upheaval, I conceived and designed a work called *Lucifer,* created for the legendary Russian dancer Rudolf Nureyev and the great British ballerina, Dame Margot Fonteyn. *Lucifer* was followed by a ballet based on Nathaniel Hawthorne's classic novel, *The Scarlet Letter.* Another piece, *Acts of Light*, was a meditation on the sun as a symbol of revival and fresh hope.

Hope for my company, I knew, meant staying current. From the wider world of dance I drew on other talents to attract a new generation. I brought in guest soloists, such as the sensational Russian star, Mikhail Baryshnikov, to dance the groom's part in a revival of Appalachian Spring.

On a playful note, I gave Liza Minnelli a prominent narrative role in a production of *The Owl and the
Pussycat.* With Tom's help, I kept my company in the
public eye, dancing well, and positioned for more funding. Among my contributors was the newly formed
National Endowment for the Arts. Decades earlier,
when I danced at the White House, I had hoped
Federal monies would encompass dance. At last they
had.

Throughout my eighties and well into my nineties,
I stayed active and productive, creating some twenty
new dance-dramas to be staged. One of these was
inspired by the melody Louis Horst used to cheer me,
many years earlier. It was, of course, my favorite Scott
Joplin tune. I called my light-spirited ballet, *The
Maple Leaf Rag.*

Once again, my company was flourishing. My
school attracted new students, and I resumed the
leadership of international tours. I had reached a point
when lifetime awards are given. In 1976, President
Gerald Ford conferred on me The Presidential Medal of
Freedom. Also in the nation's capital, I was honored by
the Kennedy Center. At each award ceremony, I felt I
represented my entire company.

I felt their appreciation for me now. They welcomed me to share their curtain calls after every one of
their performances. The dancers came out first, of
course, and took their bows, center stage. The curtain
would fall and when it went up, I would be onstage
alone to receive my own ovation.

No one saw the stage hands help me hobble out to my position. No one saw the great effort I made to stand up, unsupported, on my own. No one saw my slow and painful exits from the stage. What the audience did see was actually a performance, however brief. In this small drama, I was cast as foundress, priestess and "a force of nature."

I had it all, it seemed. I did not look like a woman who walked the floors at night, running through a litany of losses, fears, regrets. Questions snatched at me like beggars' hands. Would I leave my company secure? Or had my decisions put it in jeopardy?

Two incidents brought these into sharp focus.

Once, during a rehearsal, Annette, a fine dancer, went into a spiral fall and twisted her knee. Her curly auburn head bent in pain. Her angelic face was distorted as she cried out. She could not get up. I went to her at once; in a moment the company surrounded her.

I looked up for a moment and caught Tom in an unguarded moment. He stood aloof, watching with no expression on his face. And then, as I stared at him, Tom yawned. Annette's dance partner yelled for him to call an ambulance. Tom's face darkened. "You don't tell me what to do," he snapped. "I tell you." In the end, I called the ambulance myself.

Why didn't I talk to Tom about this troubling incident? Because that night was my birthday — he was taking me out to Le Cirque; no doubt he would present another perfect gift. How could I confront him then? The next day, he appeared in my office with a silver-framed photograph of me, performing. Again I put off the discussion. There was always some reason why I couldn't confront Tom, it seemed.

Even when he fired Annette six months later, soon after she had recovered and begun to dance again. Tom did not consult me; he simply let her go. The girl was in tears and I was in a state. The reason, she said, was Tom's opinion that she wasn't strong enough to dance without the risk of further injury.

"He didn't even give me a chance," she wept.

"I'll talk to him," I said. "It will be all right."

"No. I can't stay now. Not with him here."

"But darling, you're so gifted, we need you."

"He'll always be jealous that you like me."

"Annette, think it over, don't go now."

"I have to, Martha. How I'll miss you."

Wiping her eyes, Annette walked out.

The other dancers were upset and I had to handle it alone. Tom had to make a plane; a business trip. When he returned, a week later, there were other issues to discuss. I never had my say about Annette.

Instead, I paced my flat at night and held extended dialogues with my dressing table mirror. I realized I'd made a terrible mistake when I'd appointed Tom as the company's Artistic Director — someone who'd never been a dancer. My company had good reason to resent him. But how could I remove this man who 'd saved my life; who had given years of loyalty, attention and companionship?

The answer escaped me. Still, I realized, I'd been uneasy about Tom for some time. How much did I know about this tawny haired young man with those keen blue eyes? The most I knew about him was his affinity for tomatoes and cheese. He never talked about his past, except briefly about his education.

And yet he'd been quick to talk about intrigues in the studio. During my "dark passage," he had told me about conspiracies against me in the company. Now I began to wonder just how true they were. How many dancers had I "let go" on his advice, his "information?" I stopped my pacing, paralyzed by this thought.

Leaning against the wall of my dim apartment, I felt hot tears run down my face. Had I made the same mistake again? The kind I'd made with Erick? Had I entrusted everything — including my will — to a man who had hidden motives for his own advancement?

From the hall table, I snatched a china ashtray and hurled it to the floor. Wasn't I at an age to be wise, not foolish? How could I have woven Tom into the very fabric of my life? I must make some serious changes when our company returned from our upcoming tour.

These questions followed me on our travels. When I returned with serious pneumonia; the questions trailed me to the hospital. I demanded to go home. The questions hovered by my great Malaysian bed. I had to recover, I told myself, so I could mend what was amiss. Despite my will, I seemed to grow weaker.

I lingered a fortnight, too ill to take any kind of action. I tried to rally, hanging onto life beyond the doctors' expectations. My death, apparently a peaceful one, came as a nasty surprise.

Even then, I suspected my destination was Hades.

■

EPILOGUE

My spirit reels.

Hades holds nothing back.

Watching your entire life unfold before you is a staggering experience. It is an emotional tidal wave; you are the shore. The impact alone could kill you — a moot point in my case, of course. Even so, I am over-whelmed. Let me warn you: *Don't try this at home.*

I am flooded with a mix of gratitude and grief. A typical response, I'm told: honest, balanced, no hysteria. There is cause for great rejoicing. There is cause for deep regret. I weigh them both and ponder each. It is not for me to judge. I am here to learn. Part of that process comes next: An unexpected and unwelcome coda. Now that I have looked over my past, I must review its consequences. That's part of the cosmic package. To get this over with, I've already embarked on the final viewing. I have been eased into it with such care, I expect it to be agonizing.

First you get the positive post-mortems. The eulogies. The fond remembrances. The benefits you left behind immediately after death. I have seen my Center for Contemporary Dance: Thriving students, superb dancers, successful presentations of my work. I started to feel quite good about my legacy. Too good.

I grew suspicious. There is something more to this, I know. My spirit shrinks from this discovery. The next section begins to unfold now and it does not look promising. That initial rush of euphoria has evaporated like perfume. I want to look away but I'm compelled to watch.

Flash-forward: Ten years after my departure. Things have changed. I see a dance studio, dim and dusty and unused. An empty school, lights off. Both of these were mine, I know; I recognize them instantly. My company is in serious danger. It has lost its rights to my works. Someone else holds them under copyright now and sells the rights to those who wish to perform them.

A multi-million dollar lawsuit is in progress. My dancers fight for what is rightfully theirs. Performances are in suspension; the company's future is precarious. Two years pass. Still no resolution. This is agony to watch — and more to come. I must take a hard look at my part in what has happened.

At its root are my choices, my decisions. That old woman, pacing in the dark, was right. My life's work is threatened; my dancers cannot dance. How can I bear so much regret, such grief? No wonder we avoid the backward glance. It is more bitter than acid.

Now the recent past appears. Again I want to look away; again I am compelled to look. I see a blur at first and then a shape. This shape clarifies into a room: a courtroom, it appears. It is packed and everyone is tense, hushed, waiting. Now the black-robed judge begins to read out her decision. Her gavel comes down. The room explodes with joy — cheers, embraces, tears, applause. I wonder who these victors are and what they have to do with me. I look closer.

Of course — I recognize them now. They are my dancers, past and present, alive and corporeal. By law, my company has regained its rights to the body of my work. And I am here to view this triumph. Once again, I am overwhelmed.

More images appear to me now:

My studio begins to fill with light.

The dancers gather and approach the barre. There they bend, they flex, they stretch. They are in rehearsal for one of my last pieces, a dance of hope and regeneration: *Acts of Light.*

~~~

My review is finished

I have a great deal to ponder but I have learned this much: Hades offers you meanderings and memories. If you take on its challenge, however, there is more to come. Hades offers you a gift.

You cannot change the past — but you *can* bless the future. You can send as many blessings as you wish and they will travel far, like light, and their presence will be felt by all who receive them.

I begin now.

I have much to do.

■

AUTHORS NOTE & ACKNOWLEDGMENTS

By definition, this novel is a work of fiction, not biography. It is important to emphasize that distinction. To an author, historical fiction is always a challenge. It is particularly so when the main character's lifetime was fairly recent and she is remembered in different ways by different people.

This work focuses on the main character as a woman and is not intended to be a history or commentary on the Modern Dance Movement.

This novel is grounded on facts relating to Martha Graham, but this book is an imaginative rendering of these facts and the characters it involves. Thorough research has been the novel's foundation.

This research has involved such primary sources as Graham's autobiography, *Blood Memory*; secondary sources, most notably biographies by Agnes de Mille and Russell Freedman; reminiscences by former and current Graham dancers, especially those found in Robert Tracy's *Goddess*, and Jean Cano Bear's *Acts of Light*; films of Graham made by Nathan Kroll, as well as interviews and onsite observation at the Martha Graham Center for Contemporary Dance in Manhattan. *The New York Times*, *London Dance* and other periodicals detail the legal battle over rights to Graham's work, including the final judgment.

I want to reemphasize my gratitude to Agnes de Mille and *A Dancer's Life* and its personal anecdotes. These were extremely helpful in creating certain scenes around them.

For a more extensive list of sources, please see the Acknowledgments and Bibliography, which follow.

Characters in this novel are based on or inspired by historical people, but are not intended to be a literal representation of them. For example, the character of Graham's husband is informed by factual research, recorded interviews, and other dancer/ choreographers' impressions. In the end, though, there are private moments and gaps which leave room for the historical novelist to capture.

But the character itself is only loosely based on the historical person herself. The character's dialogue is not drawn from direct quotes and the characterization is informed by several sources, some of which conflict. The nature of the couple's altercation in Chapter Eight remains unclear, even to an onsite witness. A disastrous *pas de deux* was reported by another onsite contemporaneous witness.

The character of Tom Smith is fictitious and any resemblances to living persons is purely coincidental.

Martha Graham herself is rarely quoted verbatim Most such quotes occur in the section on her teaching and another is her ringing credo, "Wherever a dancer stands ready, that is holy ground." A list of permissions sought and granted also follows.

Unfortunately, it is impossible to depict or refer to all 181 of Martha Graham's works in one novel. I have included several dances considered to be "signature" pieces or which have special significance to Graham's life. I regret that such works as *American Document* did not fit into my concept for the novel.

Martha Graham was born near Pittsburgh, Pennsylvania, on May 11, 1894 and died in her Manhattan apartment of coronary arrest brought on by pneumonia on April 1, 1991, about five weeks shy of her 97th birthday.

Her father was an "Alienist" (the nineteenth century term for psychiatrist) who practiced in his home during Martha's lifetime. He did take the child Martha to the zoo to observe wild animals' movements and Martha continued this observation in New York.

Martha's mother was descended from the Mayflower pilgrims. The family name was Beers. Elizabeth Prendergast acted as nanny and housekeeper in the Graham household, where Martha was the eldest of three daughters.

Martha's temperament is well-documented. At ten she experienced the death of her 18 month old brother from rheumatic fever.. This was Martha's first close experience with death and her mother was devastated for a long time thereafter.

Dr. Graham moved his family to Santa Barbara, California, as the novel indicates. Ruth St. Denis's poster and performance did make an indelible and life-changing impression on Martha at age 16. The detail about the violet corsage is also drawn from factual accounts. Dr. Graham died of a heart attack in 1914.

Martha Graham did attend Comnock College and Denishawn. Her audition is based on factual reports, as is the incident about the phone, the tablecloth, and the way Graham danced her solos for Ted Shawn. Graham did leave Denishawn, move to New York City, and dance with the Greenwich Village Follies.

She lived for a brief time in a narrow one-room studio in Carnegie Hall and a bit later, in Greenwhich Village. Her relationship with Louis Horst is a fact, but many of its details and all its dialogue are imagined.

It is true that Martha asked Horst to play "The Maple Leaf Rag" to cheer her out of "the glooms" and toward the end of her life, she created a ballet to that music by Scott Joplin. The story of Graham's final trip with Horst to Wake Forest is also based on fact, as is his last birthday party, gumdrops included, and Horst's death.

The story about the costume for *Lamentation* is based on fact, as are the ballet's reviews. The same is true for *Frontier*, which Graham danced for President Roosevelt in 1937; she was the first American dancer invited to perform at the White House. One source indicates *Frontier* was on her program that night; other sources are silent on that point. Martha Graham was indeed too nervous to dine with the Roosevelts.

Martha Graham's marriage was notably stormy but passionate, as depicted here, but much of that situation must be left to the imagination. Erick Hawkins did leave Graham in London on tour.

The couple divorced and in 1957 Hawkins formed his own company and remarried. The anecdote about the poem left in Graham's dressing room is drawn from fact, as is the later incursion by a solist from another company.

Bethsabee de Rothschild was a faithful and generous friend to Martha and Martha did help establish a Graham-style dance troupe in Israel, run by Bethsabee (Batseva) de Rothschild, who emigrated from Paris to Tel Aviv in 1958.

The scene involving the Nazis' invitation to the 1936 Olympics is grounded in fact and Martha's firm refusal of their offer is accurate.

Martha Graham won many awards in her long life: The Presidential Medal of Freedom, the Kennedy Center Honors, the Handel Medallion, among them. She was also the first dancer to function as an official cultural ambassador. Some of Graham's financing did come from Katherine Cornell, Lincoln Kirstein, and Robin Howard, who was overlooked in a public tribute. The generosity of the de Rothschild family to Martha Graham is remarkable.

There was indeed tension and pressure about Martha's duration as a dancer. After several attempts by friends and critics to persuade her to leave the stage, Lila Wallace and her attorney did accomplish that mission. Martha's breakdown did occur and her struggles with alcohol are well-known and well documented. She did stop drinking cold turkey on her own and never drank again.

During the last seventeen years of her life, Martha Graham continued to teach, create new dances, choreograph them, and lecture, despite severe arthritis. She made several international tours in her eighties and nineties. However, this novel's focus is on the preceding decade.

Between 2000 and 2002, Graham's company was embroiled in a serious legal situation which caused the temporary suspension of performances. The dispute resulted in a multi-million dollar lawsuit which was settled in the dance company's favor. It is impossible to go into greater detail here due to legal considerations. The Graham Center for Contemporary Dance continues to flourish as do its teachers around the world.

Founded by Martha Graham in 1926, it is the oldest modern dance company in America in continual action. The Graham company is on a worldwide tour as I write and anticipates its annual New York Season.

Martha Graham's legacy lives on.

A note about Hades:

Martha Graham was a lover of Greek mythology and based several of her ballets on Greek myths.

Ancient Greek mythology describes Hades as the setting for the afterlife, characterized by wanderings in its mists. It is important to note that Hades does not carry the connotation of Heaven or Hell. For the novel's creative framework, I have added a bit to the original Greek legend.

I gratefully acknowledge the kindness, generosity, and assistance of Janet Eilber, Artistic Director of the Martha Graham Center for Contemporary Dance, as well as Suzanne Flanagan also at the Center.

"The Notebooks of Martha Graham," with an introduction by Nancy Wilson Ross, have been very helpful, as well as Martha Graham's autobiography, *Blood Memory.* I gratefully acknowledge both.

I also wish to express my thanks to original source material in *Goddess: Martha Graham's Dancers Remember*, by Robert Tracy; *Acts of Light* by Jean Cano Deane and John Deane; *Ballet for Martha: The Making of Appalachian Spring* by Jan Greenberg and Sandra Jordan; *Bird's Eye View* by Dorothy Bird: very special thanks to Ms. Bird for the anecdote about Ms. Graham's mother.

Very special thanks and grateful acknowledgment are due to these sources in particular: *Martha Graham: A Dancer's Life* by Russell Freedman; *The Dancer Revealed*, a film by Nathan Kroll, with footage of Graham dancing her own works; and most of all, *Martha: The Life and Work of Martha Graham*, a biography by the late choreographer Agnes de Mille who was Graham's close friend. The source material, anecdotes, and opinions in de Mille's work were extremely helpful and I offer this source particular appreciation.

I also acknowledge the helpful and consistent reporting of the Graham legal situation by *The New York Times. London Dance,* and other periodicals.

Finally, I thank the dancers at the Martha Graham Center for Contemporary Dance for their generosity of time and spirit.

Marcy Heidish
December 30, 2011

■

SELECTED BIBLIOGRAPHY

Bentley, Toni. *Winter Season: A Dancer's Journal*, University Press of Florida, 1982.

Bird, Dorothy. *Bird's Eye View: Dancing with Martha Graham and on Broadway*, University of Pittsburgh Press, 1997.

Blom, Lynne Anne. *The Intimate Act of Choreography*, University of Pittsburgh Press, 1982.

Cano, Nan Deane. *Acts of Light: Martha Graham in the 21st Century*, University Press of Florida, 2006.

Cheny, Gay. *Basic Concepts in Modern Dance: A Creative Approach*, Princeton Book Company, 1989.

De Mille, Agnes. *Martha: The life and work of Martha Graham*, (biography) Random House, 1956, 1991.

Freedman, Russel. *Martha Graham: A Dancer's Life*, (biography) Clarion Books, 1998.

Froman, Kyle. *In the Wings: Behind the Scenes at the New York City Ballet*, John S. Wiley & Sons, 2007.

Graham, Martha. *Blood Memory: An autobiography*, Doubleday, 1991.

Graham, Martha. *The Notebooks of Martha Graham*, Harcourt Brace Jovanovich, Inc. 1973.

Greenberg, Jan and Sandra Jordan. *Ballet for Martha: Making Appalachian Spring*, Roaring Brook Press, 2010.

Helpern, Alice, Ed. *Martha Graham: Choregraphy and Dance*, Vol 5, Part 2, Harwood Academic Publishers, 1999.

Horosko, Marian. *Martha Graham: The Evolution of her Fance Theory and Training*, University Press of Florida, 1991, 2002.

Love, Paul. *Modern Dance Terminology*, Princeton Book Company, 1997.

Newman, Gerald and Eleanor. *Martha Graham: Founder of Modern Dance*, Franlin Watts Publishing, 1998

Soares, Mansfield. *Louis Horst: Musician in a Dancer's World*, (biography) Duke University Press, 1992.

Thomas, Linda. From Squirt Blossom to Goddess, CreateSpace, 2009.

Tracy, Robert. *Goddess: Martha Graham's Dancers Remember*, Limelight Editions, 1996.

■

A Woman Called Moses

-Award-winning, best-selling novel based on the life of Harriet Tubman, abolitionist and conductor on the Underground Railroad.

-A Literary Guild Alternate Selection;

-A Bantam paperback.

-A TV Movie, starring Cicely Tyson, still available on DVD.

- Houghton Mifflin Co., 1st Publisher

Praise for *A Woman Called Moses*:

• *Publishers Weekly*: "Her story has been told before, but never as eloquently, almost poetically, as here...achingly real...a strong narrative of a totally committed woman, one who speaks directly to our own desperate need to feel committed — and our wish that somewhere in the world there were more people like Harriet Tubman."

• *Washington Post Book World*: "Profoundly rewarding ...a daring work of the imagination."

• *Chicago Sun Times*: "Marcy Heidish has, almost uncannily, crawled into the skin and very mind of Harriet Tubman.... The dialogue sings with poetic beauty."

• *Houghton Mifflin Co.*: "As events build toward a stunning climax on the Underground Railroad, we are drawn into the spellbinding narrative of an extraordinary life, and a portion of our American past."

Witnesses

- Award-winning novel based on the life of lay minister Anne Hutchinson, America's first female advocate of religious freedom.

- Citation: Society for Colonial Wars; laudatory reviews; large-print edition published as well as hardcover and paperback versions.

- Houghton Mifflin Co., 1st Publisher

Praise for *Witnesses:*

- *The New York Times Book Review*: " ...nothing ordinary about her creation of this remarkable woman. The novel abounds in literary grace. It employs the voices of the times as though heard this minute."

- *The New Yorker Magazine*: "A striking novel...a compelling portrait."

- *The Washington Post*: "Pure pleasure. Anne Hutchinson is real; thanks to *Witnesses,* she at last assumes her proper place...in American history." —Jonathan Yardley, Pulitzer Prize-winning critic.

- *Ballantine Books*: "This fearless woman, mother of fifteen, a leader in medicine and politics, comes to vivid life in these pages. A true believe in religious freedom who paid dearly for her principles in two trials for heresy. In the tradition of Arthur Miller's *The Crucible*, Witnesses is the deeply felt portrait of a woman in the paranoid climate of 17th century Boston."

The Torching

-Acclaimed contemporary novel, in hardcover and paperback.

- Literary Guild Alternate Selection; laudatory reviews.

- Optioned for TV movie.

- Simon & Schuster, 1st Publisher.

Praise for *The Torching*:

• ***Washington Post Book World***: "Because of Heidish's skill, we get the full force of her double-whammy...in part due to the grace with which she weaves the present-day and the historical, but also because of her inventiveness at the book's close, the daring way she gets both strands of plot to unite.... Marcy Heidish is a stylish and intelligent novelist to boot, more than up to the dizzying, tale-spinning task that she set for herself here."

• *Kirkus Reviews:* "Shuddery mystery-suspense with super-natural overtones."

• *Library Journal:* "Intricately constructed...A deliciously spine-tingling, multi-layered literary mystery..."

• *Publishers Weekly*: "Subtle and gratifying psychological suspense...Penetrating characterizations...Heidish impeccably orchestrates the historical and contemporary, the super-natural and psychological."

• *Baltimore Sun:* "Fine, goose-pimply."

• *Denver Post:* "Macabre ride...Eerie...Intriguing... Frightening surprises...Enjoy."

• *Arizona Daily Star*: "An imaginative, amazing writer... A magician with words."

• *New York Daily News*: "Compellingly readable and likely to induce the screaming-meemies."

The Secret Annie Oakley

- Acclaimed novel based on the life of the legendary sharp-shooter.

- In addition to hard- and paper-back versions, a *Readers Digest* Condensed Novel.

- Optioned for film.

- Translated into several languages, laudatory reviews.

- New American Library,

  1ˢᵗ Publisher.

Praise for *The Secret Annie Oakley:*

- **Kirkus Reviews**: "An immensely touching and cohesive fictional biography of the legendary sharp-shooter... builds from exemplary research to a fresh portrait of a talented woman in crisis...a class act—as Heidish reconstructs. with color and drama, the choreography of the shows, the tone of the period, and the textures of a haunting past."

- **The Arizona Daily Star**: "... an imaginative, amazing writer ... a magician with words.... Each character has been brought to life with a mere pen stroke; flesh and blood beings that are more than fiction.... A master-piece of creative writing."

- **The Kansas City Star**: "An unforgettable story."

Miracles

A Novel About Mother Seton, The First American Saint

MIRACLES

A Novel By Marcy Heidish

- Historical novel based on the life of **Mother Elizabeth Seton**, first American-born canonized saint.

- Main selection, *The Catholic Book Club*.

- New American Library, 1st Publisher.

Praise for *Miracles*:

• *New American Library*: "*Miracles* is the story of an unforgettable woman's life and love. It is a novel charged with the vitality of a life that saw many changes, and with the power of a love that took many forms ... [whether] as a lonely daughter of a wealthy, indifferent man; a searching young woman; a contented matron embracing a marriage that produced five beloved children; a widow searching for new meaning to life."

• *The New York Times Book Review*: "This appealing book, told from the point of view of a skeptical modern priest, moves swiftly through tragedy to triumph."

• *Kirkus Reviews:* "Working delicately with a balance of Church hagiography and psychological insight, Ms. Heidish provides another strong focus on the root dilemma of female saints and achievers."

Deadline

-Contemporary psychological novel with a "mystery" as a narrative line.

-Nominee for prestigious national "Edgar" Award; fine reviews.

- St. Martin's Press, 1ˢᵗ Publisher.

Praise for _Deadline_:

• **Washington Post**: "_Deadline_ is a tense, well-turned tale, filled with authentic police and newspaper people. Heidish's taut, punchy style moves the story at lightning speed."

• **Kirkus Reviews**: "The high-tension plot is enhanced by sharply etched pictures, by many vivid characters, and by a crisp, clean, first-person style. Heidish imbues her haunting story and her gutsy heroine with a rare sense of tenderness and poignancy. An impressive mystery by a gifted writer."

- **St. Martin's Press**: "This wire-tight novel probes relentlessly, driving deep into psychological darkness and violent death. As the riveting story reaches its stunning conclusion, we see a complex woman forced to meet the ultimate deadline."

A Dangerous Woman: Mother Jones, An Unsung American Heroine

- A compelling, inspiring new historical novel, another powerful "profile in courage" American-style novel based on the life of Mary Harris Jones, a self-proclaimed Hell Raiser, daring labor leader and colorful, quirky humanitarian

• The arresting novel of an indomitable force, dressed demurely in widow's weeds and lace collars who:

> • As an Irish immigrant – lost her homeland to the Great Famine.

> • As a wife and mother – lost her whole family to yellow fever.

> • As a dressmaker – lost home and business to the Chicago Fire

> • As a survivor – turned from sorrow to help others survive.

Follow one of America's most feisty, fearless...and forgotten heroines whose rallying cry was:

"PRAY FOR THE DEAD — AND FIGHT LIKE HELL FOR THE LIVING!"

Lightning Source UK Ltd.
Milton Keynes UK
UKOW04f0359231014

240506UK00004B/206/P